FRAGILE MEMORIES

When Maura inherits the manor house in Picton near Salisbury, she is busy living in London and working as a model. However she returns to Wiltshire to put the property on the market, Maura is overwhelmed by her memories and longs to keep the house. Sadly it just doesn't seem financially viable. Then Maura's boyfriend, Nick, offers a solution ... but would it work when her heart still belongs to her first love, Ross Edwards? Maura is drawn into a complex web of family conflict. Will she come to regret her decision to return home?

FRAGILE MEMORIES

FRAGILE MEMORIES

by

Joan M. Moules

Magna Large Print Books
Long Preston, North Yorkshire,
BD23 4ND, England.

British Library Cataloguing in Publication Data.

Moules, Joan M.
    Fragile memories.

    A catalogue record of this book is
    available from the British Library

    ISBN 978-0-7505-3504-5

First published in Great Britain in 2010 by Robert Hale Ltd.

Published in Large Print 2012 by arrangement with Hodder & Stoughton Ltd.

Magna Large Print is an imprint of Library Magna Books Ltd.

Printed and bound in Great Britain by
T.J. (International) Ltd., Cornwall, PL28 8RW

Chapter 1

'I don't understand you, Maura. Why in heaven's name do you have to go dashing off to the wilds of Wiltshire this weekend?'

'Because I want to see my inheritance, Nick. Surely you can understand that. I'd have gone last week if we hadn't been going to that christening.'

'But Anne and Pete are giving a party. They'll be disappointed if we don't show up.'

'Nonsense. There'll be so many people there they won't miss us. In any case I saw Anne in the week and told her I should be away.' She turned the fullness of her deep, amber eyes towards him, and a softness crept into her voice as she said, 'Come with me, Nick.'

'Too much work to do to go chasing something that isn't necessary. After all, you're going to sell the place, aren't you?'

When she didn't reply he said gently, 'Well, are you, Maura?'

'Yes.'

'You don't sound too sure. After all, what would you do with a crumbling old manor house? Your work, all your interests are here in London.' His arm came round her and she smiled up at him.

'I expect you're right, Nick, but I spent part of my childhood there and – well, it seems disloyal to Uncle Tom not to go and look.'

Nicholas Page laughed and moved away from her. 'How long have you lived here? Five years now, and in all that time you haven't been back. So how can it be disloyal now your uncle's dead? False sentiment, Maura, and it doesn't suit you.'

Her chin lifted in a defiant gesture, and her voice trembled very slightly. 'Maybe, but I'm going just the same. I'll be back Sunday evening. I'll phone you then.'

When he left she went into the bedroom and pulled a small suitcase from the cupboard above the built-in wardrobe. 'I shall go down on Friday evening,' she said to the empty room, 'I'll ring Mrs Duffy tomorrow to let her know.'

She had been out of the country on a modelling assignment two weeks ago when Thomas Wareham died. When she returned it was to discover that the old man had been buried the day before. 'We tried to contact you,' the solicitor told her when he spoke to her on the telephone, 'but when there was still no reply from your number after several days we went ahead with arrangements. He had, in any case, left explicit instructions.'

He had also left her the manor house. That *had* been a surprise. She would have expected her cousin Jim in Canada to have inherited it. Even though he had quarrelled with his stepfather all those years ago, he was still closer family than she was.

It was true what Nick had said, that she hadn't been back to Picton since her move to London five years ago when she was eighteen, but she had seen Uncle Tom a couple of times every year when he came to town for one of his board meetings. He had been against her modelling career at first. 'You're mad,' he'd said in his forthright manner. 'Modelling isn't the glamorous life you think it is, you know. With your secretarial training you could get a good job in Salisbury, have your own suite of rooms here at the manor...'

But she had known that wouldn't work. Not with Ross so close. Ross Edwards was the reason for her leaving, after all. Yet she had never returned even after Ross emigrated. Vividly now she recalled Uncle Tom telling her that Ross had gone to Australia. 'He came in for a drink before he left, got a job on a sheep farm out there. I shall miss him,' he'd said, 'he's good company.' And she had turned away so he wouldn't see how even the mention of Ross's name could affect her.

She left the suitcase in the corner of the bedroom and went to have a shower. This time tomorrow night she would be back at the manor. The manor without Uncle Tom, and without Ross. It would seem strange, but she knew she must go just once more before she sold the place and laid the final ghost. How Nick would laugh at that. She had met him four years ago when she had been one of the models in an extravaganza he'd organized for the opening of his restaurant in the West End.

At first she had been one of many girl-friends, but gradually it had been Nick and Maura and no one else. She didn't delude herself that he never flirted or took out another woman, but she believed him when he said it meant nothing.

'And it's in your power to prevent it,' he'd told her more than once. 'We could be married, or just set up home together and it would stop. But until you agree to it, then I'm still an eligible bachelor.'

She stepped out of the shower, slipped into a blue-towelling robe, and ran her fingers through her long, dark hair. She supposed that one day she might marry Nick. He was exciting, ambitious, handsome, and he loved her. Yet whenever he pressed her for a decision she hung back. 'Why change anything, Nick? We're happy enough as we are, we have a lot of fun, don't we? If we were together all the time it might not work as well.'

'What are you afraid of, Maura?' he asked one night, in a rare mood of sensitivity.

And she wasn't able to tell him because until then she hadn't analyzed it herself. But when she did she knew that it was the memory of Ross that held her back from any other emotional commitment. The memory of that time between her seventeenth and eighteenth birthdays. The memory of when she was in love with Ross Edwards, and she had believed he was in love with her.

I was young and vulnerable then, she thought, and it was a wild infatuation, not the real thing at all. And surely now was the time to confront those fragile memories. Perhaps it was best that Nick wasn't coming. Going back to Picton alone would be good for her. And once the manor was sold she'd have no ties there at all, and nothing to return for.

She woke in the early hours of the morning, sobbing into a pillow already wet with tears. Liberally splashing her eyes with cold water later, she realized that it was the first time since learning of her uncle's death that she had really let go. The first time for many years she had thought about that wonderful summer when she was seventeen. She was realistic enough to know that most of her tears were for that shattered dream.

This weekend would sever her last remaining ties with the area. On Saturday morning she would go into Salisbury and instruct an estate agent to sell the manor and its contents for her. Then she would think about a future with Nick.

It was a beautiful sunny morning. The window box was cheerful with the brightness of the daffodils she'd planted, and the weather forecaster on the radio said it would be a warm weekend. Maura tidied the flat, added a cotton dress to the clothes already in her suitcase, checked her appearance in the long mirror in the hall, and prepared to leave for work. The telephone rang as she reached the front door. It was Nick.

'Come over to my place tonight, eh, Maura? I promise I won't keep you up late so you'll be fresh for an early start on Saturday morning.'

'I'm going down tonight, Nick. I'll probably go into Salisbury to see the estate agent on Saturday.'

'Yes, of course. Well, have a good trip, then. Don't bother to ring on Saturday night because I shall be at Anne and Pete's party.'

She had almost forgotten that. 'I won't,' she said. 'I'll wait until Sunday.'

When he rang off she wondered if it would have occurred to her to telephone him anyway, and she thought it probably would not have done. She could survive forty-eight hours without Nick, although perhaps this wasn't a happy state of affairs in the case of someone you were thinking of spending the rest of your life with.

She was booked for a nail-varnish advertisement Friday morning. For once everything went smoothly and by 2.30 she was finished and free until Monday afternoon. Back at the flat she showered and changed, picked up her smart leather weekend case, went downstairs and into the busy London street.

She enjoyed much about living in the

13

capital, and for the purposes of her work it was necessary. If I lived in the country again I should miss the theatres and art galleries, she mused as she drove through a maze of back streets to avoid the worst of the traffic and get herself on to the road that would take her home. It wasn't until she was clear of London and bowling along towards Andover that she realized she still thought of the manor as 'home'.

Picton looked smaller than she recalled, and as she drove slowly through the village, over the narrow bridge, she was aware of a hollow feeling inside her. She had been a very immature teenager when she left, now she was a reasonably sophisticated young woman of twenty-three, with a career and a salary that gave her the opportunities and independence she enjoyed.

As she turned the corner into Fieldspar Lane the manor came into view, its centuries old stonework looking soft and mellow in the warm spring sun. Maura took a tremendously deep breath as she swung the wheel of the car sharply into the drive.

'It was very quick,' Mrs Duffy told her that evening as they sat together in the warm kitchen after she had sated her appetite with homemade steak-and-kidney pie washed down with half a pint of cider. 'He complained of feeling unwell late in the afternoon – thought it was a touch of indigestion. He went for a walk to clear it, then to his room for a nap. "I'll be all right by dinnertime, Mrs Duffy," he says to me, "so don't let me sleep too long. Call me ten minutes before you're serving."'

Sniffing and dabbing her eyes, she said, 'I did, miss. I went up and tapped on his door and when there was no answer I knocked louder. I was going to leave him then, thinking the sleep would do him good, but he'd said not to let him sleep too long and you know what he was like, miss, if you disobeyed his orders, so,' her voice caught on a sob and she swallowed hard, 'so I went in and – and poor Mr Wareham was lying there on his back looking for all the world as if he was asleep, but I could see at once that he was dead. He looked just like my Harry did when he went, miss. I touched him, just to be sure like, but he wasn't in this world any more.'

Maura said, 'I'm glad it wasn't a long-drawn-out business for him. I'm only sorry I was out of the country. If I'd known I'd have flown straight back.'

'Wouldn't have done the old gentleman any good, miss, not by then it wouldn't, but I know what you mean. But he had a nice funeral. Most of the village turned out. What about you miss, will you be coming back to live here now?'

Maura prevaricated. The whole village would know she was selling if she told Mrs Duffy, and she wanted to keep it private a bit longer. It was obvious to her that she couldn't keep the manor unless she did something with it. Although not a large place, it needed more upkeep than her compact flat, she thought humorously. In any case all her contacts for work were in London.

'Not immediately,' she said. 'I've a lot of modelling commitments for the next few months, so I shall need to stay up there.'

Aware of Mrs Duffy regarding her solemnly, she added, 'But I expect I'll be down quite a bit to go through everything, sort it out. In between assignments, you know.'

Deftly she changed the subject, but during the entire evening no mention was made of Ross Edwards by either of them. Maura didn't ask because she thought Mrs Duffy would surely say if there was any news of him. Although that lady couldn't possibly know how very much the new owner of the manor house longed to hear a whisper of that once-beloved name. Perhaps it was just as well, she thought wryly, as the housekeeper filled her in on most of the local gossip.

There were six bedrooms in the house, and Maura was in her old one which overlooked the lawn and rosebeds behind the house. Of course, the roses weren't out now, but gazing down from the window she felt a peace and well-being from simply being back. She had always loved the place, right from a small child when she visited with her parents and had the run of the grounds, provided she didn't damage any plants. From this window she could glimpse the roof of the summerhouse where, years ago, she had played and pretended it was her very own home. And where, later, she and Ross had kissed...

She was just thirteen when her parents died, both killed in a head-on car crash when a vehicle travelling towards them went out of control. She attended a day school in those days, but when Uncle Tom stepped in and took charge he sent her to a boarding school in Kent. But her holidays had all been spent here, and although he was a brisk and rather peppery uncle she grew extremely fond of him. He was strict but always fair. It wasn't until she was eighteen that she learned that he wasn't her official guardian. She had presumed he was because he took over, paid her school fees, gave her an allowance and, more important, a home.

She moved from the window and gazed around the familiar room. How often during those first months in London had she dreamed of this place. The shelves which still housed her books and ornaments, the curtains and wallpaper she had chosen, the pictures that adorned the walls. Dear Uncle Tom, she thought. It must have been a lonely life for you after I left, yet you never tried to get me back on that score.

He *had* tried to stop her from leaving, though, and it was one of her great regrets that they had quarrelled so bitterly when she went. That was when she learned he wasn't legally her guardian. She sat on the edge of the bed now and seemed to hear his voice again after all the shouting had finished.

'Of course I can't prevent you going, you're almost eighteen. And seeing the mood you're in now, *asking* you is no use.'

She saw again her young self, defiantly facing the power of him, 'I shall go whatever you say or do. You can get a court order if

18

you like, but it couldn't be enforced until you found me, and I would make sure you didn't. London's a big place to hide in.'

'I couldn't get a court order, Maura. I'm not your official guardian, you know, nor your wicked uncle trying to keep you here against your will, for all that you think I am.'

'Not – not my guardian? Then who is?'

'Nobody. When your parents died they – well I suppose they just weren't prepared for something like that to happen. They thought they had years of life left. There was nobody else, your grandmother was too ill...'

'You mean you've educated me, and, and looked after me all these years sort of un-officially?'

She remembered he had smiled, a sort of twisted half-smile when he said, 'That's about it, Maura. And I've enjoyed most of it, too. But you've always been your own woman. I confess I wondered how it would work, me taking on a thirteen-year-old young lady, but if I hadn't, the law would have stepped in to find you somewhere to live. As it is you're free to go whenever you wish. I do ask you, though, to let me know where you are, for my peace of mind.'

How young and hurtful I was, she thought now. Yet he forgave me and always came to visit. *And* bought me the flat as an eight-eenth-birthday present. I wish I could have been here when he died, wish I could have told him I loved him.

The birds' serenade woke her early the following morning, and it took a few moments to realize her surroundings. She went down to the kitchen to make a cup of tea and Mrs Duffy appeared while she was drinking it.

'Did you sleep well, Miss Maura?'

'Fine, thanks. Much better than I expected to.' She smiled at the housekeeper.

'I'll see to your breakfast then. How would you like your egg?'

Maura walked over to her, 'Nothing cooked, thanks. Just some toast and cereal. And don't bother about lunch for me. I want to go into Salisbury later so I'll have something there.'

She walked round the grounds after breakfast, then systematically through all the rooms. She would need to see the solicitor as soon as possible, but he probably wouldn't be there on a Saturday morning. The estate agent will, she thought, so I'll get that hurdle over today.

She loved Salisbury. 'It's one of my favourite cities,' she had told Nick once, and he immediately wanted them to drive down one Sunday, but she refused. It was too close to home and Ross was still in the area then.

Now she wandered round, looking at the river, watching the swans and ducks, and finishing by buying some fruit in the market, knowing she was only delaying the moment when she would put the manor up for sale.

I'll have a coffee then see about it, she thought, turning into a café. She chose a corner table where she could watch the bustle of the busy town, and as she slowly sipped her drink she admitted to herself that now she was here once more she didn't want to sell the property. The five years' absence melted away and at that moment she would have given up everything else to be able to keep the manor. But commonsense told her it was impossible. She couldn't afford to live there without a job, and all her contacts were in London. If I did find something here it wouldn't be modelling, and anyway the manor is much too large for me alone.

What about Nick, an inner voice said, and she tried to picture him there, but she couldn't. He was essentially a town man – why, he had even wondered what she would find to do for two days in the country. Unbidden, images floated into focus: Ross standing by the fireplace in the drawing-room, Ross sitting with her at the big scrubbed table in the kitchen and sampling Mrs Duffy's ginger cake, Ross ambling round the garden... She drained the last drop from her cup and rose to go. This simply would not do. Ross was in Australia, he was in the past. The present was Nick. She was going to sell the manor and return to London to marry Nicholas Page. She would probably become very involved in his restaurant business and eventually give up modelling, especially when they had a family. She had survived five years without seeing the manor, after all.

The spring sunshine gave a continental look to the city. One optimistic restaurant owner even had some tables and chairs with bright sunshades over them outside on the pavement. She stood for a moment watching the bustle and colour of the market place, and then along the road came the brewer's dray, the lovely shire horses and their driver looking as though they had stepped out of a picture postcard. She felt glad they were still about, delivering to the pubs in the city. It gave her a feeling of security just when she needed it. They were a well-remembered scene from her childhood. Slowly she walked towards the estate agent's office.

The agent, a Mr Toning, said he would come out tomorrow when she explained that she had to return to London on Monday morning. 'No problem,' he said to almost everything she mentioned. Certainly no problem to sell the manor.

She returned to the car park feeling low. Heavens, woman, it isn't sold yet. Even now you could go back to his office and tell him you've changed your mind.

But she knew she wouldn't. It had to be a clean break. She had built herself a new life – it was a very satisfying life and she must acknowledge the fact that coming back here had reawakened old memories, nothing more. She was a different person now from the eighteen-year-old girl that Ross had known. He would have changed, too, in five years. Had probably married the farmer's daughter Uncle Tom told her about some time ago.

She reached her car, unlocked it and placed her bag of fruit on the front seat next to her. Come on, Maura, she said silently to herself, this isn't like you. You've done what you came to do, now go home and sort out what you want from the house, then leave the agent to get on with it.

As she inserted her ignition key she became aware that she was being watched by someone in the vehicle parked next to her. Turning her head she looked directly into Ross Edwards's eyes.

For a few seconds she thought she was having an illusion, that her thoughts during the morning had made her imagine it was Ross. Then he moved, swiftly stepping from his car, and she saw there was a woman with him. A woman with honey blonde hair and sky-blue eyes sitting in the front passenger seat. It was too late to move away, Ross was already tapping on the window. Slowly, as if in a dream, she wound it down.

'Maura, by all that's wonderful.'

'Hullo, Ross,' she said, surprised to find her voice sounding almost normal.

'I can hardly believe it.' His eyes devoured her. 'When did you get back?'

Just as though I'd simply been away for the weekend, she thought. 'Last night. Did you know Uncle Tom died?'

'Yes. I'm sorry, Maura. Look, we can't talk here – can we go somewhere for coffee. You don't need to dash off now, do you?'

She didn't mean it to, but her gaze went towards his car and the woman sitting in the passenger seat. He looked too. 'That's OK,

Jane's in no hurry. Come on and I'll introduce you.'

'*No*. I mean, I'm sorry, Ross, but I really do have to get back. I'm expecting an important telephone call from London, and I have so much else to do.' She pulled her seat belt round, but he was still standing there. 'Perhaps another time,' she said quietly. 'Now, if you could just move to give me room to get out–'

'When do you return to London?'

'Monday morning, or – I might have to go tomorrow.'

He grinned at her, that sudden impish grin she recalled so well, 'Right, see you then.' He blew her a kiss as he moved away from her wheels.

She stopped on the road back to Picton and pulled into a lay-by to get her thoughts in order. She had been prepared for a traumatic weekend but not a face-to-face meeting with Ross. Why hadn't someone told her he was in England again? Although I've only spoken to Mrs Duffy and the estate agent, she thought. The agent wouldn't know it mattered, and Mrs Duffy just might not know he was here. Tomorrow, if she went to church, would be the time when she would hear all the news.

A thousand questions chased themselves

around in her brain. Was he back for good, or simply on holiday? A business trip? A honeymoon? It really shouldn't concern her any more, she had abdicated that right five years ago, and he had accepted her abdication without a fight. Wearily she rubbed her hand over her eyes, took a deep, deep breath, and concentrated on the rest of the run home.

Maura had been indoors less than fifteen minutes when Mrs Duffy came panting upstairs.

'There's someone to see you, miss,' she said.

Turning from the bookcase where she had been sorting through her books, and trying to decide which ones she wanted to keep, she ran her hand through her hair. 'I didn't hear the bell. Who is it, Mrs Duffy?'

The housekeeper lowered her eyes. 'A gentleman, miss; he says it's urgent business.'

'I'm busy just now. Oh, all right, show him into the drawing room. No wait, I'll come down,' she said, suddenly, realizing it might be Mr Toning, the estate agent, being discreet by not stating his business. Although she wasn't expecting him until Sunday morning something could have cropped up. Smoothing down her dress she preceded Mrs Duffy through the door and down the stairs, mildly surprised when the housekeeper indicated the kitchen, and not the small study leading from the hall.

She was aware of Ross as soon as she entered the kitchen, although she couldn't see him because of the column which supported the great archway across the middle of the room.

Standing absolutely still she said quietly, 'What do you want?'

He came round the structure and walked towards her. 'To talk to you before you disappear again. Don't look so frightened, Maura, I won't eat you, though you look tasty enough for sure.' His big wide smile was so easy, so relaxed...

Suddenly she found her voice. 'Why have you come? We've nothing further to say to each other, Ross. Sneaking in like that, too – what did you do, bribe Mrs Duffy not to say who it was?'

He pulled out a chair and sat down, 'Something like that. Told her I wanted to surprise you. She said she had some chores to do in the other room anyway. Well, aren't you going to sit down too, Maura? This is not exactly the warmest greeting I've had since I've been back.'

She walked over and sat down facing him. 'What did you expect? That I'd throw my arms around you and say how I've missed you this last five years? Well, I haven't,' she rushed on. 'I've been far too busy carving a career for myself.'

He reached over and lifted both her hands into his. 'Too busy for marriage too, I see.'

Angrily she jerked her hands away. 'That's none of your business, Ross. Now get to the point and say what you came to say.'

'I came to see you, to tell you that I had missed you. Oh, I've been busy too, but not too busy to miss someone who is an important part of my life. I reached Britain last week, to find Tom was dead and buried, and when I enquired about you they said you hadn't been down, not even for his funeral.'

'I was out of the country. I didn't know, it was very sudden. Do you think I'd not have come otherwise ... oh,' she rose and pushed the chair roughly away from her, 'why should I defend myself to you?'

'Why indeed. I hadn't flattered myself that you stayed away because of me, Maura.'

She heard the telephone ringing in the hall and the murmur of the housekeeper's voice.

'You had better go now, Ross. I daresay

that call is for me.'

'That's OK, I'll wait.'

The audacity of the man, she thought, casting him a swift glance as he crossed his long legs and smiled imperturbably at her.

She nearly knocked Mrs Duffy flying as she almost ran through the door.

'A Mr Nicholas Page on the phone, miss.'

'Thank you.'

He sounded loud, almost brash after Ross's deep tones. 'How are things, Maura? The old homestead still standing?'

She knew he was joking, but it was the wrong time for her. 'Of course,' she snapped.

'Have you seen an agent and set things in motion for getting rid of the place?'

'You're very anxious about that, aren't you, Nick?'

'Naturally I am. I know you pretty well, Maura, and you follow your heart rather than your head over these emotional things. Seeing it again might make you swerve in what you intended to do. These old properties need a lot of keeping up. Do remember that if you're tempted, darling.'

Crossly she said, 'Just go to the party and leave me to sort things out here, will you, Nick?'

'Of course I will, my sweet, but you can't

29

blame me for feeling concerned about the girl I'm going to marry. I need her here with me. Together we can do great things in the restaurant business. You know we can.'

Sighing, she said, 'Is that all you rang for?'

'Now don't be awkward, Maura. I rang because I'm missing you. Have you seen the agent and are you coming home tomorrow?'

'Yes to the first and probably no to the second. But I'll be back on Monday morning, I've a modelling session in the afternoon.'

That's the second man in ten minutes to say he's missed me, she thought as she returned to the kitchen.

Ross was gazing out of the window. Without turning he said, 'Nicholas Page. The name rings a bell. Is he your current beau, or your steady one?'

When she didn't answer he moved from the window and came towards her. 'Maura, if I hadn't ... found you ... so unexpectedly in the car park this morning I should still have been here, you know. I intended to come again and ask for your London address–'

'Please go, Ross. There is no point in all this. I don't know what your plans are, whether you're returning to Australia or staying in England, but when I leave here after this weekend I – I doubt if I shall ever

30

come back.'

He reached for her hand, imprisoning it with a strong grip. 'Of course you will. I've always known you couldn't stay away from the manor for ever.'

She tried not to enjoy the excitement the touch of his flesh against hers produced, but it wasn't possible. The sensuous warmth of his fingers entwined round hers set all her pulses trembling and she didn't try to pull her hand away from his.

'Come out to dinner with me tonight, Maura. We'll go to Salisbury to...'

Slowly she shook her head, anticipating the restaurant he was going to suggest, 'No, Ross. We can't put back the clock. Our lives have moved on.'

'What in heaven's name is that supposed to mean? You used not to talk in riddles. Is this what the high life has done for you?'

His hand tightened on hers. 'I appreciate that you need to return and fulfil contracts, sort out commitments, but there's nothing, absolutely *nothing* to prevent us from having a meal together. Whatever this Nicholas Page is to you – and you haven't answered my question about this yet – tonight you're here, I'm here and–'

'I'll answer your question, Ross,' she interrupted, looking down at their still locked hands. 'Nick is my boyfriend and we are going to be married.'

Chapter 2

Ross relinquished his grip, and gently stroked her fingers before releasing them completely.

'I suppose it was a lot to expect, that you would be waiting,' he said. 'Yet from my correspondence with your Uncle Tom I got the impression there wasn't any special man in your life.'

Her eyes sparked at him, and her voice was high with the emotion she was trying to hide, but she looked directly at him. 'So you discussed me, did you? It was all right for you to go off to Australia and lead your own life, but not for me. What made you think you had a right to know, anyway? Just because we felt romantic about each other once doesn't mean we still do. And I'm not the sort of girl to...' Before she could say more Ross pulled her towards him and kissed her with a passion and fire that left her in no doubt of his feelings at that moment.

When they eventually drew apart his fingers ruffled her hair in the well-remembered way, and he murmured, 'Maura, Maura, you wanted that as much as I did. Oh, my darling, my dearest, say you still love me as I love you.'

She felt dazed by the overwhelming flood of feeling that she had been powerless to prevent as she returned his kiss. Moving back a couple of steps to put a few inches distance between them, she tried to regain the hard-won composure that had taken countless days and nights in the early years of her self-imposed exile to achieve.

But he moved with her, throwing his arm round her shoulders and turning her towards him. Once more his lips sought hers, and although at first she tried to hold back, it was impossible and for a few moments she abandoned all inhibitions and savoured the full ecstasy of being in Ross's arms again.

He was the first to pull away this time, and the quiver that ran through her body as he moved was like the tearing of a perforated edge. She knew she had to be strong, there was no future here for her with Ross, it was too late now to salvage what they once glimpsed. His marriage was in the way, and if he was planning to return to Picton, the sooner she left the better it would be for them all.

'It's no use Ross, it – wasn't meant to be. Go home to – to Jane,' she forced herself to say the name of the woman she had briefly seen in the car this morning.

'To Jane? Whatever for? I don't live with Jane.'

For a few seconds her heart soared to the heavens, but her joy was short-lived. So Jane wasn't the sheep farmer's daughter Uncle Tom had said Ross was marrying. But someone was.

Deliberately she turned away so he wouldn't see the desolation she felt. 'I'm going back to London early Monday morning, Ross, and Nick and I will be married just as soon as this place is sold. Now please leave, I – I have a lot to do and–'

Roughly he caught her arm and swung her round to face him. 'Sold. *Did you say sold?* Since when has the manor been up for sale? And in heaven's name why?'

'Ross, you're hurting me. Let go.'

He did so abruptly. 'Is that where you went this morning – to put the manor on the market?'

Nodding miserably she turned from him, but he pulled her back into the circle of his arms, and this time the only passion she saw in his eyes was anger.

What would have happened had Mrs Duffy not appeared to announce the arrival of Eleanor Poole, Maura wondered, later that evening. As it was she turned thankfully toward the housekeeper. 'Ask her to come in, please. Ross – Mr Edwards, is just leavng.'

For a moment she thought he wasn't going to move, then he strode forward, his long legs reaching the door in a couple of paces. 'I am,' he said, and the grimness left his face to be replaced by the lazy smile she had loved so much, 'but I'll be back.' Briefly his hand touched hers, re-igniting the burning tremors she was trying to control, 'and so will you, Maura, *so will you.*'

He spoke pleasantly to Eleanor Poole as they passed in the hall. 'I heard Ross Edwards was home,' she said to Maura as she clasped her in a warm hug. 'He's looking fit. Now, how about you, my dear? It is good to see you again. You stayed in London far too long.'

Suddenly conscious that they were still in the kitchen Maura apologized and took her guest along to the drawing room.

'I understand you were abroad when your

uncle died. He was well liked you know. The village will miss him, but it will be nice to have a young element at the manor again. Once you have settled back properly I'll organize a small dinner party, my dear. Now, shall we see you in church tomorrow?'

When Mrs Poole left, with the promise that the new owner of the manor house would indeed be in church the following day, Maura went back to her bedroom and returned all the books to the shelves. This wasn't a job she could rush, and she realized now that she would need to come down again. She could make lists and work everything out on paper first, then spend a few days here to implement them. She hoped Ross wouldn't say anything about the proposed sale of the manor, but no way will I ask him not to, she thought. It's a chance I must take.

Sleep that night was a long while coming. For the first time for many years she did not push away the memories; instead she let them come in full flood, seeing again in her mind and heart the young girl she had been that year she fell in love.

'Sweet seventeen and never been kissed,' someone had remarked at the party Uncle Tom gave for her birthday. Amid the friendly laughter Ross had led her on to the dance floor, whispering as soon as they were out of earshot, 'We will certainly have to remedy that, Maura.' He had danced her round twice before expertly steering her through the ballroom door and on to the hotel veranda. 'Still too public,' he muttered and, taking hold of her hand, had almost whisked her down the steps and into the grounds. There, beneath a weeping willow by the lake he'd taken her in his arms and kissed her.

'Well,' he said, releasing her mouth but keeping a firm arm round her waist.

'Well what?' she'd enquired, breathless from the excitement his kisses had roused in her. It was hard to believe that this was Ross Edwards whom she had known for years.

'Let's do it again, my little princess.' She had pushed him away, angry at the patronizing tone of his voice.

'I may be years younger than you Ross, but I'll have you know that I *have* been kissed before.'

'Like that?'

Remembering the clumsy, fumbling of two previous young suitors against Ross's deeply satisfying attentions, she knew exactly what he meant. Nevertheless, she wasn't going to boost his ego when he still treated her as a

37

child, or at best as a very young adult.

'Every time and every boy is different.' She hoped she sounded as experienced as he obviously was.

Then suddenly she was in his arms again and caught up in a swirl of ecstasy as his mouth rained kisses on her lips, nose, cheeks, eyes, and in the hollow of her throat. She had never known anything as sweet, never felt anything as stirring, never wanted anything as much. Her responses startled her as much as him.

After that night they were inseparable. Ross at twenty-five had studied farm management and was about to put into practice what he had learnt. He was due to take over the management of a small farm two miles from Picton the following week. She had opted to leave college and not try for university which had been a disappointment to both her teachers and her uncle, she recalled now. But she had known what she wanted to do since she was twelve. Be a model, wear chic and glamorous clothes and frequent the restaurants and haunts of what seemed to her a most interesting lifestyle.

Of course she knew now that it wasn't, but she had been happy in her chosen career. She had worked hard and earned a great deal of money, although for the first few years, if it hadn't been for Uncle Tom, Maura acknowledged to herself, life would have been much harder and bleaker. As it was she would never encourage a daughter of hers to pursue the same career.

What was she thinking of? A daughter. She and Nick weren't married yet, maybe they never would be. In spite of her remarks to Ross, and her fondness for Nick, deep in her heart she was doubtful about making a marriage work when one partner was not completely in love with the other. And she knew that no matter how much she disguised her feelings to herself, she did not, nor ever could, feel for Nick the powerful emotions she had once felt for Ross. She had thought, had hoped, that returning to Picton would exorcise his memory, but even before she knew he was back the ghost of his presence had been haunting her. And now it was threatening all she had worked and fought for.

She slipped into church with just a few moments to spare the following morning. That at least avoided too many questions before the service. During her absence from Picton the old vicar had retired, so she was a stranger to the present incumbent. He welcomed her enthusiastically as she came out, and soon she was overtaken by Eleanor Poole and had to endure the embarrassment of reintroductions among her friends. Some were new to her, but many she remembered, although several of them no longer recognized her. As Mrs Anstruther-Jones remarked, 'You went away a young girl and you've returned as an extremely beautiful young woman.'

She escaped as soon as she could, relieved that Ross hadn't put in an appearance. She hadn't expected him to; he was seldom there in the old days when she dutifully went with Uncle Tom every week when she was home, yet she had found herself surreptitiously watching for him.

Back at the manor she had an early lunch, then gave Mrs Duffy the afternoon and evening off. 'I've lots of sorting out to do,' she said, 'and I'm perfectly happy to make my own tea. I've not been used to being waited on for the last five years, you know.'

'Well, if you really are sure, then I'll pop along to see Sarah.'

'How is your daughter, Mrs Duffy?'

'She's fine. Got another baby you know, a year old come middle of next month. A little girl, ever so pretty she is.'

'I'll take you over in the car,' Maura offered, glancing at the clock. The estate agent was due to arrive in three quarters of an hour.

'I wouldn't hear of it, miss. No, don't you worry, I'll go on my bike like I usually do. It's a lovely day for a ride and it'll do me good.'

She seemed to fiddle around after that for so long that Maura thought she would still be in her quarters when Mr Toning arrived, but she left ten minutes before he came, and Maura breathed freely again. Of course people would get to know the manor was for sale, but she would rather it was later than sooner.

Mr Toning was smooth. There was no other word for him. He went through the house with her, making notes and periodically nodding his head until she longed to slap it into stillness. He looked out of place wandering about in the grounds, immaculately dressed, clipboard in hand. It has to be done Maura, she told herself, once this bit is over you can do anything else by phone.

When he left, promising to deal with everything personally, she walked in the garden herself. It was in good order, Uncle Tom had

41

employed old Bill who lived in the village for years. He had always been completely in charge of the garden. 'You put in what you think will look right, Bill,' she remembered Uncle Tom saying on more than one occasion. 'I'll soon let you know if I don't like it.'

She walked now beyond the main lawn, to where clumps of daffodils were planted beneath the shelter of the trees. The garden had always been a joy when she was home, from the first delicate snowdrops and primroses, the abundance and colour of the polyanthus, the scent of the wallflowers, the beauty of the summer roses and lavender bushes through to the glory of the autumn chrysanthemums and Christmas holly.

Ross had walked in the garden with her so much ... there she was, doing it again, thinking about Ross when for the last five years she had done her damndest to forget him. Perhaps she should come with Nick next time. She followed the curving path to the summerhouse. This wasn't in such pristine condition as the rest of the house and garden. Definitely needed a coat or two of paint, and a bit of restoration, she thought, trailing her hand along the dusty bench and gazing through the rather smeary windows.

'Maura.' His voice startled her and she

turned sharply.

'I did ring the bell but when there was no reply I thought I might find you here.'

'I told you to go away and stop bothering me, Ross. I'm busy, I've a thousand things to do and I can't have you popping in all the time as though you owned the place.'

In two strides he was by her side. 'That's a good one, coming from you, Maura. If I had the money I *would* buy the place, but I haven't, so that idea's out of the question. What I can't understand is why you're selling up. You could run your career just as easily from here as from London. Or is it this boyfriend,' he almost spat the word at her, 'who wants you to do it...?'

'It's none of your business.'

He ignored that. 'Tom loved the manor and he thought you did, too. We often talked about it—'

'Get out,' she said, dangerously quietly, 'I do not want to know how you and Uncle Tom discussed me when I wasn't here.'

'You make it sound as though it was something nasty, but believe me, Maura, it helped us both. He loved you so much and he knew I did too. He told me he was going to leave you the manor eventually. "Jim hasn't any feel for it," he used to say, "but

43

Maura has.'"

Maura wasn't sure afterwards how it happened but suddenly she was shouting at him and pummeling her hands against his chest, and he gripped them, one in each of his large strong ones.

Then, bending his body towards her, he kissed her hard and bruisingly on her lips.

'You beast, let me go, let me *go*.'

'Not until you've heard me out,' he answered, so calmly she wondered how it was possible after that kiss. 'We never "discussed" you in that sense, but we talked about you often.'

'You had no right to. I expect you encouraged him to tell you things. How would you like it if someone talked about you behind your back? You're despicable, Ross Edwards, as highhanded and full of yourself as you ever were.'

'And you're just as prickly.' He took his hands away so suddenly she jerked backwards and almost fell, and although he didn't laugh aloud the amusement showed in his eyes and she saw it.

'It's a good job we didn't marry after all,' she threw at him, turning her back so he wouldn't see the tears she could already feel welling into her eyes. 'I even feel sorry for

44

your wife, having to put up with your over-sized ego. Just go now and leave me and the manor alone.'

'I will.' He stormed out, and she willed herself to hold on until he was out of earshot. Her breath was coming in little gasps and then his voice was there again, behind her.

'What wife?' he said, 'I haven't got a wife.' When she looked round he had gone.

Chapter 3

Maura left for London early the next morning and the thought of Ross not being married persisted. Uncle Tom had told her on one of his visits last autumn that 'Ross is getting married after Christmas'. He hadn't said how soon after and perhaps that was why he was here, possibly planning a spring wedding. 'It's nothing to do with me,' she told herself sternly. 'He and I were all washed up five years ago.'

Back home in the flat Maura wished that she didn't have a modelling assignment this afternoon. And a date with Nick this evening. More than anything else just now she wanted to be alone and think about the situation. What situation, she asked herself silently? Nothing has changed really. The fact that Ross isn't married to anyone else hasn't altered your life or plans. She seemed to hear his voice again: *You're just as prickly, aren't you?* Yet now, without him so dangerously close to set her heart thumping, she could even smile a little at that remark, and at her reaction to it. If she was to be absolutely frank with herself there was more than a grain of truth in it too.

The modelling session was for dresses for a catalogue. She had worked for them before, with the blonde who was also booked for this afternoon. They liked to have one blonde and one brunette, it made the pages of the catalogue more interesting.

The phone was ringing as she inserted her key into the lock on her return. She raced upstairs and reached it the moment it stopped. 'Damn!' She kicked off her shoes, went to the cabinet and poured herself a drink. Time to get back to realities; it was probably Nick, anyway, to check that she was back. And who else would it be, she asked herself, trying to find some humour in the situation. Not likely to be Ross, and if it had been I'd have probably told him to leave me alone. But the thought of Ross persisted, the thought that he hadn't married after all.

When the phone rang as she stepped out of the shower, she threw on a bathrobe and hurried to answer it.

'You're back then, sweetheart,' Nick's voice was caressing. 'I'll be round in half an hour. Put on your prettiest dress, we're going to Ciro's.'

Later, dancing cheek to cheek with Nick, and feeling him hard against her, she knew no sense of joy, no rush of excitement, yet when Ross had simply held her hands this morning in the summerhouse it felt as though the stars had left the sky and were all around her.

They had a table on the side, away from the edge of the dance floor, and when the band struck up again Nick leant towards her. 'Let's sit this one out, Maura. I want to talk.'

She looked at him beneath the soft lighting. At the smooth evenness of his features, not exactly handsome, but attractive, especially when his blue eyes sparked with enthusiasm for a new project. What was it this time, another stunt to bring even more diners to his restaurant? She knew he enjoyed dreaming up ways to be different from the others.

'Is the manor up for sale now, darling?'

She took a long while to answer, and was conscious of him straining to keep quiet and not rock the boat.

'Yes it is,' she said eventually.

'Good. I do know how you feel, Maura. You probably won't believe that but it's true. To start my business I had to sell an inheritance I would rather have kept. I've never told you that before, have I? I've never told anyone that before.'

She reached across the table and touched his hand. 'Did you, Nick?'

He nodded and brought his other hand to rest on hers. 'I haven't regretted it, though. It was the sensible thing to do because this is where my work and interests were. As I hope and believe yours are, Maura.'

He squeezed her hand very gently.

She smiled at him. 'Nick, get to the point will you. What wonderful scheme have you in mind for Nick's Palace next?'

He eased his hand from hers and reached into his pocket. 'Not for the restaurant, Maura, for you my dear – for us. I think we've prevaricated far too long.'

He was holding a small blue box towards

her. 'Go on, open it.'

'But Nick...'

'I know; you'd like to have chosen it yourself, but if I wait for that day we'll both be drawing the pension. And I want you now, Maura, I want you beside me all the time, not just some of it.'

'No Nick, not yet, not tonight.'

'Open it, Maura. If you don't like that one I'll change it, we can select something to-gether...'

His fingers closed over hers, and lifted the lid. Inside was a large emerald flanked by two only slightly smaller diamonds. Even in the dim lighting of Ciro's the ring shone and twinkled like green fire.

Swiftly he took it from its velvet nest and reached for her hand. 'We can be married by special licence and live in the flat over the restaurant while we look around for a more suitable place. There, it fits perfectly. I knew it would, my darling, because I had several sizes sent and tested them against that little one you wear on your right hand.'

Mistaking her look of incredulity for approval, he said, 'Crept into your bedroom when you were in the shower a couple of weeks ago. I knew that ring would be on your dressing table...'

Maura pulled the emerald from her finger, and with slightly trembling hands, replaced it in its box.

'I know you want us to be married, Nick, but I won't be rushed. I'm not – not sure if I'll ever get married, actually. I like being on my own. It's been great this last few years, but if you need something permanent perhaps we'd better call it a day and leave you free to look elsewhere.' In silence he reached for the box and replaced it in his pocket. His eyes, steely blue now with anger, gazed at her.

'I'm sorry, Nick. I really am.'

'It's that manor house, isn't it? You've been different ever since you knew. You surely don't want to live there, do you?'

'Of course not. I've already told you it's up for sale. Let's go, Nick.'

They drove back in silence, stopping at the restaurant on the way. 'I'm expecting an important message, they were going to page me at Ciro's with it,' he said. 'Are you coming in?'

'Yes, I left my scarf here. I need it for a job tomorrow.'

She went upstairs to Nick's private apartment to which she had a key, while he was talking to reception. She collected the scarf and a favourite pair of shoes she kept here and was just closing the door when Nick came up. 'That's not necessary, you know.' He almost snatched the shoes from her. 'We can go on as we were. We're mature people, aren't we? We'll forget this evening happened. I guess I jumped the gun a bit, but I thought all girls still wanted the romance of an engagement and wedding ring in spite of all this women's lib business. Obviously I was wrong.'

'It isn't that, Nick, it's something in me. I admit, going back' – she almost said going home – 'has unsettled me a bit. Seeing it all again...'

'Of course.' His arm came round her shoulders. 'I should have given you more time, but I missed you, Maura. I suppose I was half-afraid that once you were there again you wouldn't return.'

She moved her head a little so she could see his face. 'But you knew I would. There's my work...'

'Your work is very important to you, isn't it?'

'You know it is.' It has to be, she thought, it's one of the reasons Ross and I quarrelled.

'But you won't be able to go on modelling for ever. I imagined that when – if – we were

51

married you would come into the business with me. You've learnt such a lot about it these last few years and together we could do even more than I already have.'

'Let it ride Nick. I'm – honoured that you asked me but–'

He placed his hand gently over her mouth, 'Don't say it darling, don't say no while you're feeling like this–'

'Like what?' Her words came out more sharply than she intended, but for once Nick didn't rise to the bait. Instead he gently squeezed her shoulder and said, 'Unhappy. It's never a good time to make a decision. It's my fault for broaching the subject tonight, and clumsily too. I'm so besotted over you I didn't think. Come on, I'll take you home.'

With his arm still about her they walked down the stairs to the foyer of the restaurant. 'I'll just tell reception I won't be back to-night, darling.' As he walked away she was conscious of someone watching her and, turning slightly, she found herself gazing straight into Ross's dark eyes. He inclined his head. 'You always seem to be leaving as I arrive.' Then, mimicking Nick's tone he added, 'Darling.'

Ignoring the sarcasm in his voice she said, 'What are you doing here?'

'Well, it is a restaurant, so I'm planning on having a meal, then I...'

Nick rejoined her. 'Ready, my love?'

'Yes. Nick, this is Ross Edwards. Ross, Nicholas Page.'

'Good to meet you,' Ross said. 'I've heard the food and service are excellent in your restaurant.'

'You've not eaten here before?'

Ross shook his head. 'I've been in Australia for the last few years. Only returned to Picton last week.'

'Picton. Near Salisbury?'

'You know it?' Ross said, and Maura knew he'd deliberately mentioned it to rouse Nick.

'Only slightly. Our business keeps us here in town a great deal. Come, Maura, we'd better be on our way.' He held out his hand, 'Enjoy your meal, Ross. I'm sure you will. Our chef is among the best half-dozen in the world.'

Nick didn't mention the encounter until they were at Maura's flat making coffee. 'Ross ... what did you say that chap's name was?'

'Ross Edwards.'

'Well, thanks for recommending Nick's Palace to him. An old school chum of yours, is he?'

'No. Just someone I knew when I lived in Picton. And please, next time I introduce you to a friend, don't say *we* in that proprietary tone, Nick. It's your restaurant, your chef, not ours.'

'Did I say "ours"? Wishful thinking, darling. Anyway, I don't suppose Ross whatever his name is would think anything about it. He could see we were together anyway.'

She banged the delicate cups and saucers on to a tray and tried to keep calm. Until Ross had re-entered her life so suddenly last week she had felt reasonably ... reasonably what? Happy, content, satisfied? Yes, satisfied. Was it Ross or was it that the manor was her inheritance, her real home, and she was loath to give it up?

Almost as though he read her thoughts Nick said, 'I'm about ready to expand the business again, perhaps we should look at your manor house to see what possibilities it has.'

'Possibilities?'

He smiled, and she knew again why she was the envy of half the girls in their set.

'As a restaurant.'

'The manor as a restaurant?'

'Why not,' he said. 'I hadn't thought to go

out of London but it might be a good idea to have a country restaurant. Could be the Glyndebourne of the catering world. The Rolls Royce of eating establishments.'

'Oh Nick, you're not serious. Are you?' she added softly.

He took the tray from her, 'Of course I am. You should know by now that I never say what I don't mean.'

'But a restaurant – your kind of restaurant in Picton?'

'Why not? People there need to eat and I imagine some of them eat out. If we can attract them to our place they wouldn't have the problems of parking in Salisbury, or anywhere else, and,' she heard the excitement mounting in his voice, 'the locals could drink and walk home. Yes, it's definitely an idea worth looking into. Have you any photographs of the place?'

She drank her coffee, then went into the bedroom, returning with a small dark-blue suitcase. 'There will be some of the manor in here,' she said, 'but I'm not convinced it would be a viable proposition.'

She had put the case on the floor and was sitting on the deep-pile rug to open it. Nick squatted beside her now and leant over to plant a kiss on the tip of her nose. 'I shall look into the matter thoroughly, my sweet, but I've a feeling in my bones that it will be just right. I can see the advertisements now – oh nothing brash. I'll dream up a suitable slogan and name. Nicholas's Manor Restaurant for classy food in classy surroundings, something like that.'

'Nick, you're going too fast...' she was rummaging through the stack of photographs in the case to find one showing the whole of the manor house, and her mind was suddenly full of ideas. Maybe she could keep the manor if it were to be run as a business. 'Here,' she said, handing Nick a print of the front of the house.

'Mmm. Certainly imposing, the sort of place where people will like to dine as long as the food's good, and we shall make sure it is. Let's go down and see it as soon as possible, Maura. Meanwhile, fill me in with some data about the village and the surrounding ones. I think advertising a place like this in the right quarters will be the thing to do here. Local trade wouldn't bring in enough. We shall need a gimmick – an upmarket one, I grant you – but something to encourage people to make the trip to Wiltshire from various locations.'

She was still looking in the case for suitable

photographs, and found one showing a different view. 'This was taken from the back, Nick. You can see some of the rose garden here. It's a picture all through the summer. Uncle Tom loved his roses and took great pride in them.'

He took it from her. 'Of course we should need a gardener or two, and we could make the rose garden into an outdoor section. Yes, I think there are possibilities in this idea, don't you?' He leaned across her and took a handful of photos from the case.

'Hey, look at this one. Is it you? Yes, I can see it is now, but how very young you look. Very pretty and fresh. A sort of "before life has touched me" picture. Charming.' He passed it to her and as she studied it she smiled, 'That was taken on my sixteenth birthday. I haven't looked at these for so long.'

Nick flicked through the bundle in his hand, pausing every now and then to look closer at some of them, while she sorted a few more taken both inside and outside her old home.

'Wow,' Nick said, 'look at this one, then. First boyfriend, eh? Oh, it's that chap we saw tonight, isn't it? Ross whatever his name was.'

She snatched it from his fingers. 'Yes it is, and there's no need to be so patronizing about how young and innocent I looked then. I was very young. Even you weren't always so suave, were you?'

His arm came around her but she pushed it away. 'Maura, I'm sorry. I was only teasing, my dear. I didn't expect you to take my words to heart like that. Of course if we looked through some of my old snapshots you'd laugh – so would I. Photos taken with gangly girls whose names I can't even remember now, but who at the time I thought were the last word. Come on, put them away and let's make plans for visiting the manor.'

Long after he left, with bad grace because he had expected to stay, as he sometimes did, Maura lay in bed unable to sleep. It wasn't the first time Nick had asked her to marry him, but never before had he produced a ring. It seemed almost an ultimatum to her. Then there was this new business of turning the manor into a restaurant. An upmarket restaurant. She smiled to herself. Dear Nick, he became so enthusiastic, but she knew he wouldn't go into it lightly. If he thought he could make a go of it he would spare nothing and no one. She had little doubt he could do it if he set his mind to it. She thought now that it was partly his ambition and get-up-and-go attitude that had attracted her in the first place. And, of course, he could usually make her laugh. Strange, she mused to herself, it was ambition that split Ross and me, but it was ambition that drew Nick and me closer.

She liked the idea of running the manor as a restaurant, and thought it could well be a paying proposition. 'I wish I'd had the idea first,' she said aloud.

They went to Wiltshire the following weekend. Meanwhile Maura rang the estate agents in Salisbury and asked them to withdraw the manor house from sale. 'At least for the time being,' she told Mr Toning, 'I may have plans to live there after all. I'll be coming down in a few days. I'll look in and see you.'

Nick didn't mention the emerald engagement ring and neither did she. He was so full of his latest project, the Manor House restaurant. 'Maybe that would sound better than "Nicholas's Manor Restaurant",' he suggested as they journeyed to Wiltshire the following weekend. 'Mustn't appear too flamboyant to begin with, not in a small place like Picton.' She smiled but refrained from commenting. Nick's business sense she trusted, he'd proved it with past successes, at first ploughing the money back into the business, and later expanding and putting managers into his restaurants. He had three now, two quite small, and the big West End one, Nick's Palace. She knew how much he liked his name included in the titles, how they'd both laughed over the fact that Nick's Café, a modest little sandwich bar and Nick's Palace, the glass-and-chromium building in the West End of London that was his pride and joy, were the same firm. In between, of course, was Nick's Place, a cheap and cheerful eating-house with plastic tablecloths, two hardworking waitresses, and a reputation for quick service. He must have had quite a tussle within himself to have decided to leave his name out of this one, she thought, but only said, 'I think that would hit the right note, Nick. Who do you see running the restaurant? I mean, you wouldn't want to be tied to a country place, would you? You've often said you couldn't live anywhere but London.'

'Depends. Certainly I'd start it off, but you're right, we could put a manager in after a time. I'll know more when I've seen it. And of course you and I would be equal partners—'

'No,' she said, surprised at the speed and vigour at which the words came from her. 'No, Nick. If you buy the manor and get planning permission for change of use, I'll run it for you. You can pay me a salary. Or, I will keep the manor house and you can rent it for the restaurant. Either way it will be a business arrangement. It's got to be until we see if it works.'

'If what works, the restaurant, or you and me, Maura?' His voice was harsh, his hands gripped the steering wheel hard and he kept his eyes fiercely focused on the road ahead.

She was silent and after a few moments he said more gently, 'You and I worked perfectly well until you were left this legacy. It seems to have unsettled you so much. To me it was simple. Sell the house. You obviously didn't want to and the other alternative is what we're looking into now. That way you'll keep your childhood memories, your roots, and we can have a thriving business too. I have some money which can be spent on this but with you and me together it can be spread out. And once we're married it will be the same firm anyway.'

'Let's wait until we've assessed the potential more thoroughly, please,' she said, suddenly close to tears. 'So far all this is conjecture.'

'If you like, but you won't be able to put off the decision too much longer. I'm ready for expansion and if this isn't it I shall start looking elsewhere. I'll be sorry if we can't do this thing together though. You and I make a pretty good team. It's not been bad for the last four years, has it?'

He did turn his head to look at her this time. 'Has it, Maura?'

'It's been great, Nick, but you know I've always said I needed to be independent. I–'

'Don't let's argue,' he said suddenly. 'This is the first time I've been to your old home. I'd like it to be a happy time. In spite of the fact that you never came near the place for years it obviously means so much to you. I didn't realize this until recently. I'll strike a bargain with you, Maura. I won't mention marriage all weekend if you'll agree to seriously consider a business partnership. OK?'

'All right, Nick.'

They entered the village soon afterwards. 'Straight through, over the humpbacked bridge, then first right into Fieldspar Lane,' she directed. She was holding her breath as he came too fast over the bridge and swung round into the lane. She realized it was

62

excited anticipation as her eyes feasted again on the ancient and well-loved house.

'This it?' he asked, as he drove through the open gates and roared up the drive.

'Yes. Leave the cases, we can get them later,' she said, her spirits miraculously lightening. 'We'll go round to the kitchen because I expect that's where Mrs Duffy is, preparing a feast for us.'

'Aren't I worthy of the front portals?' he asked, half laughing and half serious. 'No matter, we'll save Mrs Duffy's legs if that's your wish.' He was looking about as he followed her round the side of the house, where she rapped on the door and called out, 'It's me, Mrs Duffy,' before opening it and rushing in.

At first she didn't see Ross sitting by the large scrubbed kitchen table. Anxious to make Nick feel immediately at home she introduced him to the housekeeper, then, half turning, she jumped visibly. 'Ross. My goodness you startled me.'

He rose. 'Sorry, Maura. Didn't mean to. I just called in to find out what time you were arriving, and Mrs D here had the kettle on. I'll leave you to settle in and see you tomorrow.' He held his hand out to Nick. 'Good meal I had in your place the other evening,' he said, then he was gone and they heard him whistling as he went down the drive.

Mrs Duffy bustled around them. 'I'll make a fresh pot of tea, won't take a jiffy.'

'We'll have it upstairs, Mrs Duffy,' Nick said, 'I'll fetch our cases. Which way from here, Maura?'

She waited until they were upstairs in the main hall, then she chided him for being high-handed. 'Would it have hurt you to drink a cup of tea in the kitchen, for goodness' sake?'

'Of course it wouldn't, but I'm keen to see the rest of the house, not to hobnob with the servants.'

'Oh, sometimes you're insufferable, Nicholas Page,' she retorted angrily. 'I'll find out which rooms we're in.'

Before he could reply she had returned to the kitchen. As she entered from the downstairs hallway she heard Mrs Duffy talking, then Ross's voice said, 'Thanks Mrs D you're a pal.' He was gone before she reached the door.

'What was Ross Edwards doing here?' she asked.

'He came back to ask me to give you this note, miss.' The housekeeper pulled an envelope from her voluminous apron pocket.

Maura took the tea tray. 'It's all right, I'll see to this,' she said.

Nick was prowling around looking for her. 'At least our rooms are next door to each other,' was all he said when she showed him where they were to sleep.

She declined to go with him to explore the grounds. 'I'll have a shower and change. If you'd like a drink there's a cabinet in the dining room. Help yourself.'

When he had gone she pulled the envelope from the inside of her skirt and slit it open. The note was brief.

MEET ME IN THE SUMMERHOUSE AT SIX THIRTY TOMORROW MORNING. I LOVE YOU. ROSS.

Chapter 4

After dinner Nick took a large pad from his briefcase and began sketching how the Manor House restaurant would look. 'It needs a lot of work, but together we can make it *the* place to dine.' He flicked the pad over and drew a line down the centre of the next page. He headed the two columns

65

ADVANTAGES and DISADVANTAGES. Under advantages he wrote rapidly, No competition, close to a well-populated and tourist cathedral city, Grounds sufficient for outdoor eating. Under disadvantages he wrote, Kitchen downstairs, would need dumb waiter or lift large enough for trolley hotplates–

Maura leaned across to see what he was doing. 'Well?' he said, when she made no comment.

'I'm thinking. I suppose the drawing room would be the main restaurant?'

'Yes. You'd get twenty tables of varying sizes in there with no overcrowding. It would take twenty-five, but this is the sort of place to be exclusive. An archway into the library next door. That's a spacious room – I paced it out this afternoon. With the shelves down it would give you a good–'

'You mean you'd knock the wall down and extend into the library?'

'Of course. It's the logical thing to do. The little study leading from the library could be the office. From there you or I would be able to know how things were going. The panelled walls in both rooms are perfect. The colour scheme would need to be carefully planned. A royal-blue carpet maybe,

66

that's a good colour for most tastes. Not garish, yet dark enough not to need continual cleaning, and bright enough to be cheerful. Royal-blue tablecloths with a white overlay – or we could alternate and have every other table with pink cloths. No, on second thoughts we can have the pink cloths in the garden restaurant, pink is more of a summer colour.'

Maura said, 'The upstairs would stay private, wouldn't it?'

'Not sure, love. The main bedroom would make a perfect function room and as it's not over the restaurant itself we shouldn't need to worry about noise.'

'Stop, Nick. You're going much too fast.'

'Nonsense. These are only ideas, a skeleton of a plan to be honed and worked until we have it as we want it. This is a great place, Maura and it will adapt very well.'

She noticed the change from *would* make, *could* be, to *will* adapt, and a vision of Uncle Tom and herself in the library, of Uncle Tom in the little study, puffing contentedly at his pipe, came into her mind. Later, Nick went for another walk round, 'I want to make sure most of this is possible, and check the wall between the drawing room and library again. It's not a main wall, but check twice and do it once has always been my motto.'

She declined to accompany him, on the pretext of feeling more than usually tired. 'OK, sweetheart. I'll work on this for a while when I've finished my walkabout.' He flipped the notepad. 'This place has definite potential. It could yet be the crown in Nicholas Page Enterprises.' He kissed her quite gently on the forehead. 'I'll look in on you later.'

Maura made for the kitchen when he had gone. 'That was a lovely meal, Mrs Duffy. Thank you.'

She went into the garden before retiring and wandered through to one of her favourite spots, the summerhouse. No way am I going to meet Ross tomorrow morning, she thought, he must be mad to even suggest it. Everything seemed to be happening so fast. Only last week she had been prepared to sell the manor and sever her links with Picton, and now Nick was roaming around the place deciding which walls to pull down and Ross...? Hurriedly she rose from the bench. Ross didn't love her, he would never have waited five years if he had.

She pretended to be asleep when Nick looked in, not even stirring when he gently kissed her forehead. Her years of producing the right look and reaction for modelling took over, yet when the door had softly clicked she knew that had it been Ross he wouldn't have been fooled, he would have known instinctively that she wasn't asleep.

She tried not to think of Ross, yet found herself remembering vividly their parting and the reasons for it. Once more she seemed to hear his voice, quiet and authoritative. 'I want a wife who will be a partner, who will be here when I come home, not careering around the world on modelling assignments.'

And her own passionate, uncontrolled reply, 'You don't want a wife, Ross Edwards, you want a doormat.' He had reacted angrily then, grabbing her by the shoulders and turning her round so their lips were but a fraction of an inch from each other. 'You *know* that's not true. You'll have as much independence as you want. I'll never try to stop you doing anything, but modelling isn't the glamorous career you think it is and when I marry I want my wife to live with me *all* the time, not just for odd days. My work is here. If you want to model in this area, that's fine by me—'

'What chance do I have of a modelling job in Picton or even in Salisbury? That's a ridiculous thing to say.' Maura covered her face with her hands as she seemed to hear the old arguments around her. Her own angry voice beating into Ross's deep tones. Then there had been the business with Uncle Tom. At the time it had seemed that everyone she loved was ganging up against her achieving the dream she had her heart set on.

After a restless night she rose early, well before six, but did not pull the curtains nor go near the window. I can be just as determined as you, Ross Edwards, she told herself grimly. She began to sort through the books on the many shelves on each side of the mantelpiece and soon had two piles on the floor. One to keep and one to give away. The small claret red leather book of Elizabeth Barrett Browning's poetry made her catch her breath. Ross had given her that on her sixteenth birthday. A soft tap on her door half an hour later was quickly followed by Nick's presence. She only just had time to slip the slender volume beneath a larger book, then he was beside her.

'Whatever are you doing down there, Maura?'

'Just sorting through a few books. Did you sleep well?'

'Not bad. What time's breakfast, then? We

have a mass of work to do if we're to get this restaurant off the ground in time for an autumn opening.'

Maura laughed in spite of her panicky feelings. 'Nick, these things take time.'

'I know, but now we've decided we need to get going quickly. As I see it you will have the best of both worlds. You'll keep your manor house in the family and we'll have what I'm convinced will be a lucrative business into the bargain. Come on, I'm starving.'

She finished her toast and marmalade while he was still eating his eggs and bacon and, on the pretext of a breath of fresh air before joining him to look at the latest plans he had roughed out, she left the dining room. It was a little after eight now and thinking the coast must surely be clear, she went straight to the summerhouse. There was an envelope on the seat. Inside was a single sheet of paper and on it Ross had written. *I mean it*. A quiver of pleasure ran through her body as she took the note and returned to the house.

They spent the morning looking at and talking about the ideas and plans Nick had set out for the restaurant. 'I'll take care of the business side of things and you will be the hostess, the one on show, seeing the public. Could even put on a fashion show once the place was established; you have all the right contacts for that. Yes, this is what we've been waiting for, Maura, the Manor House restaurant will be different. I can see it now, classy, no brash lettering, the car park in the front and the garden section at the back. Discreet luxury. People will pay good prices for delicious food and lovely surroundings and that's what we shall give them. Eventually we might even be able to have a swimming pool in that rather rough area where the summerhouse is.'

'Oh no,' she said, 'you wouldn't pull the summerhouse down?'

'Why not? You must admit it's a bit of an eyesore, but fortunately it can't be seen from the house, so it can wait until we are rolling. But it has possibilities, Maura. A covered-in swimming pool, and a set of decent, comfortable changing rooms where the summerhouse is now.'

She was appalled, but he went on enthusiastically, 'It's different, original and in this setting the Manor House will come alive. Folk who want to swim will come into the bar afterwards and spend more than if they simply came for a meal. The pool will only be available to our clientele of course, and no children will be allowed in any part of the complex. It will be a meeting place for discerning people. Later we could even turn a couple of the bedrooms into an art gallery.'

'Nick, we have to live here. We shall need space too. A restaurant is fine, but all these other things–'

'There are six largish bedrooms, Maura, plus the library and odd studies as well as your Mrs Duffy's present domain. It's perfect for us and within two years I reckon we'll be able to put a manager in, a local man who already has a house here or in Salisbury, and we can return to London permanently.'

Maura fell silent. Of course at present this was conjecture and she realized that much of it might never happen, but she suddenly felt afraid that instead of a simple restaurant serving good food in delightful surroundings, which she had envisaged at the beginning when Nick first mooted the subject, it was already getting out of hand. Yet without running it as a business there was no way she could afford the upkeep of the manor. The money Tom Waring left her would not be enough to live there in the long term without supplementing it. There was a lot of renovation needed. She loved the place so much but she couldn't ignore what she saw as she walked round the estate. It did need a great deal of money spent on it, whether it stayed as a home or became an upmarket restaurant and another feather in Nicholas Page Enterprises.

'Maura, where are you? I swear you've not heard a word I've said this last five minutes.'

'Ooh, sorry, Nick. I was daydreaming. What were you saying?'

'That we need to talk finance, Maura. Find out how much alterations and modernization to turn it into a going concern will cost. The kitchen will be one of the biggest expenditures but it does have the enormous advantage of being large and when we strip it out we shall have the space to put in all the ovens, rotisseries and what-have-you that we need. Bags of room for fridges and freezers and lots of working areas. But none of that will come cheap and all of it will be necessary. So we need to check out how much we shall have to play with when you get your money through.'

'There won't be masses of money Nick. Uncle Tom's fortune was in the bricks and mortar of the manor, and a couple of pensions that died with him.' She did not add that he had left a few hundred pounds each to an old friend who lived abroad, to Mrs

Duffy who had been his housekeeper ever since Maura could remember, and to Ross. Ross also got his music collection and she herself a couple of nice old rings, a Victorian brooch and the balance of the money after everything had been paid. Plus, of course, the manor estate with all that went with it.

'Well, we need to get it straight, so let's go and see the agent. Find out what the place is worth as it stands. I doubt I could buy it outright but as we'll be in it together that won't matter. But we shall need to draw up legal documents of course. You've got property and I've a reasonable amount of cash and plenty of collateral. They can soon check out that the other restaurants are all doing good business. Shouldn't have any problems there.'

Mr Toning, the estate agent, was out viewing a property, so they went for lunch at one of the many inns in the centre of Salisbury first. Maura wasn't really hungry in spite of a scrappy breakfast, but Nick relished his meal, noting as they entered the place that meals were only served at lunchtimes there.

'Ours will be lunch and evening meals,' he said, 'and on the special occasions like New Year, Valentine's Day, Mothering Sunday, birthdays, weddings and so on we'll pull out all the stops and really stage a wonderful evening. People will pay for the right kind of service in our gorgeous surroundings.'

He was smiling as they walked back to the agent's office, and, tucking his arm into Maura's he said, 'Right, now for business.'

After nearly three quarters of an hour with the agent they left, armed with pages of notes about building permissions, change of use, and a list of addresses and telephone numbers. Mr Toning walked to the door of his private office with them and they both saw Ross sitting by one of the desks in the outer office in conversation with the young lady. He didn't turn round, although Maura was sure he knew they were there.

Chapter 5

Two weeks later Maura had four consecutive days free of engagements. She decided to spend them sorting out the manor.

'I'll come down if I can,' Nick said, then with a huge grin he added, 'Mustn't neglect the bread-and-butter lines for a dream, eh? Anyway it will give you a chance to chase up the permits and what have you that we need. As soon as we have everything like that sorted we can make a start.'

'Yes, but you can't rush these things, you know, Nick. It all takes time to go through.'

'So you keep saying, but you have to keep these people on their toes. There's too much red tape for my liking,' he said, 'but I don't think there'll be any problems. It's not as though it's a listed building or anything odd like that, and all our alterations will be in keeping with the place.'

Her emotions were very mixed as she drove to Picton: enormous relief that the manor would not need to be sold after all, but misgivings about the project they were planning. With his usual enthusiasm Nick seemed to be going way over the top and she was worried. She thought the restaurant idea was good; certainly she could not afford to keep the manor unless it was put to use earning money. And she knew now just how much she wanted to keep it. When the subject had first been mooted she thought it would involve the downstairs only. The drawing room as the restaurant, perhaps some rustic benches and sunshades in the garden during the good weather... She switched on the radio in the car – there would be time enough to ponder the whys and wherefores during these next few days. Nothing was firm yet, after all, and although it was to be Nick's money that would pay for the conversion if it came off, the property was hers and she would have the final word.

The manor was splashed with a pale sunshine when she arrived about four o'clock in the afternoon. Mrs Duffy, who had been in charge of the kitchen ever since Maura's memories of the manor began, was there to greet her. 'It's so lovely to have some life around the place again,' she said, then quickly checked herself, 'I didn't mean it like that really, miss, just that there was a rumour that you were going to sell the place and not come here to live, but you are, aren't you?'

'I hope so, Mrs Duffy. It's simply a question of money, you see. If I can cope with the upkeep there's nothing I want more than to keep the manor on, but–'

'Well, if a cut in my wages would help, miss, I shan't mind. Mr Tom was generous to me when he was alive and I'm well catered for so to speak. I don't need much really, but I do love this place too. It's like a second home to me I've been here that long and I'd hate to see it go to strangers.'

She turned towards the stove. 'I hope I've

not spoken out of turn, Miss Maura. I'll get on with the meal now.'

Maura walked up to her and softly touched her arm. 'Not at all, Mrs Duffy. I appreciate your concern and believe me you will be the first to know should I decide I can't keep it on. But there may have to be some changes, you see. So much needs doing, the poor old manor is really crumbling away. I – we have plans and if they come to anything it will stay in the family, I promise you.'

Mrs Duffy turned from the stove. 'Do these plans include the gentleman who was with you last week, Miss? Mr Nicholas Page?'

'Y-es, they probably do.'

Mrs Duffy returned to the stove, 'Thank you for telling me, Miss,' she said quietly, and Maura had the distinct feeling that Mrs Duffy did not approve of Nicholas Page.

Ross telephoned just after six o'clock. 'Would you like to come over for a drink?' he said.

'Just me, Ross?' she queried softly.

Did she imagine the slight hesitation before he said, 'Of course not Maura. Bring your boyfriend too, if he's with you.' She knew from the inflection and tone of his voice that he was aware that Nick was not in Picton.

She was tempted to refuse, yet the chance to talk to Ross alone over a friendly drink beckoned. Unless Jane was there, of course. She didn't know where the blonde fitted into the picture. Ross had said he didn't live with Jane but very little else about the girl. She was young and beautiful, but since that day in the car park Maura hadn't seen her, with or without Ross.

'I won't be able to stop long. Mrs Duffy is planning a cooked meal for later.'

There was a definite chuckle in his voice as he said, 'In that case come post haste – and Maura...?'

'Yes, Ross.'

'How about asking Mrs D if she could make the cooked meal stretch for two. Tell her I'll bring the wine and anything else she needs.'

'We'll see. She may have something that won't easily adapt, so don't bank on it, Ross.'

She changed into the green chiffon dress she had packed in case there was a chance of socializing during her stay. It was simple and very romantic and she knew the colour suited her well. 'You are a fool, Maura,' she said to her reflection in the dressing-table mirror as she brushed her dark-brown hair and caught the sides up with a pair of diamante clips. Fastening the amber necklace and earrings Uncle Tom had given her for her seventeenth birthday, she remembered Ross's words on that special evening. 'It's beautiful, Maura, but your eyes are lovelier still. There's magic in their amber depths.'

Mrs Duffy was happy enough to stretch the meal for two. 'It will be a pleasure,' she said, 'I'll do an extra couple of spuds for Mr Ross any time. We both missed him, your uncle and me, when he went off to Australia.'

'Was he here much?' Maura asked.

'That he was. Whenever he could get away from the farm, miss. Was a good friend to Mr Wareham. It was a bit lonely here for him on his own, and Mr Ross used to come and they'd talk and sometimes play chess. Lovely man, is Mr Ross; you tell him there's plenty of food, he can have as much as he wants.'

Ross lived at the other end of the village in Primrose Cottage. It was larger than it appeared from the outside, having three bedrooms and two decent-sized rooms downstairs as well as a kitchen and bathroom. Outside was a narrow but long back garden and a smaller front one. His father had left home when Ross was two and he had no recollection of him at all, but Maura knew he remembered his mother with great affection. 'She was so beautiful,' he once told her, 'she looked as if she had stepped out of a Gainsborough painting and was a bit bewildered by the real world. She was very delicate and that's why we lived with my grandmother, who was as robust as they come. She managed the house and food and looked after both of us. She did the garden and even managed a part-time job in Salisbury after we lost Mum and I was at school.'

When his grandmother died from a heart attack when Ross was twenty she left him Primrose Cottage and her money. 'It was a shock, her dying so suddenly,' Ross said. 'She had always been there and she'd always been strong. I hadn't expected her to go for many, many more years. I thought about selling up and going to Australia or Canada, but I was already committed to agricultural college and I'd always known I wanted to work on the land so it seemed sensible to get my qualifications.'

Maura thought about all this as she drove over that evening.

'Sherry, martini, white or red wine...'

'Hold on Ross, I'm driving remember. Perhaps a small sherry.'

He poured her a large one. 'You can drive us back then, and I'll walk home when the time comes. That is if I am invited to share your meal, of course.'

'Mrs Duffy said it would be all right. It will be ready about eight.' She didn't think it necessary to tell him how the housekeeper had extolled his virtues and was obviously an adoring fan.

'Good old Mrs D. She really is a treasure. You're fortunate to have her to look after everything for you, Maura.' He moved to the settee and patted the place beside him. 'It doesn't cost to sit down, you know, and I promise I won't bite.'

She laughed. 'I was just thinking it's so long since I've been in here but it hasn't changed. It's a lovely, homey place, Ross.'

'As is the manor house of course. What's your flat in London like?'

'You know I live in a flat then? It could be a house, a bungalow, hotel, hostel...'

'I'm not guessing. Tom told me you had a flat but not what it was like.'

Perhaps it was the sherry, or simply the cosiness of being here with Ross again, but she didn't snap at him this time for discussing her affairs with Uncle Tom. Placing her glass on the small wine table he had put in front of her she said quietly, 'It's not very big. A sitting room, kitchen, bedroom and bathroom. The sitting room's the largest and even that would fit several times into the library at home. I missed the space at first and did feel very boxed in, but I grew used to it. And of course I'm out a great deal working and away a lot too.'

'Yes, you've seen a bit of the world these last few years, haven't you, Maura?'

'I've been to many exotic places, Ross, but I've not seen a lot of them because I've been working. Fly there, work right through the day and sometimes the evening too if they needed moonlight shots on the beach in an evening dress. Ludicrous really. Tumble into bed dead beat at the end of it all because you need to be bright and smiling for the next session. Eventually fly home. One location gets to look very like another in the end.'

'Have you enjoyed it, Maura?' He put his hand over hers and she let it stay.

'Yes I have. I still do. How about you, Ross? You've travelled too.'

'Only to one place, Australia, and I didn't have time to explore it all because I too was working, you know. Although I did have a few weeks going around before I came home.'

'Are you – are you going back?'

'I don't know. Possibly. It's a great country. Farming's very different there from in England of course.' He moved his hand from hers and said quickly, 'Should we be off if we are to do justice to Mrs Duffy's food, do you think?'

She had worn a light, short coat over her dress and as he held it out for her his hands touched her shoulders through the thin material and she shivered with pleasure.

'Are you cold, my love? You can borrow one of my sweaters if you like.'

She restrained him from dashing upstairs to fetch one. Dear Ross, she thought, I could have worn jeans and T-shirt and he wouldn't have noticed the difference. But his next words showed her he had.

'You look absolutely stunning, you know, quite bowled me over when you came in. No wonder Nicholas what's-his-name enjoys taking you around. You sure about the sweater now?'

She nodded, surprised he hadn't realized how his hands touching her had sent that shiver of pure pleasure throughout her body.

He handed Mrs Duffy a small carrier bag with two bottles of wine, one red and one white in it, and told her softly, 'There's a bottle of your favourite sherry in there too – that's for you Mrs D. Enjoy it.'

'Ah, one of Mrs D's famous steak-and-kidney pies,' Ross said, as he cut into the succulent portion on his plate. He indicated the wine; they had both opted for the red. 'Shall I do the honours?'

As he poured she compared his approach to Nick's. Nick would never have asked, he would have taken charge automatically. Not that she had minded but it was pleasant to be treated with old-fashioned courtesy.

'Penny for them,' Ross said suddenly.

'My thoughts are worth far more than that.'

He handed her the glass, 'I'll tell you mine for nothing, Maura. I was thinking how lucky I am to be dining this evening with the most beautiful model in Britain, who also happens to be the girl I love.'

'What nonsense you talk,' she said lightly and without looking directly at him.

'You think so? But I told you the other day I meant what I said in that note. Never mind, I won't embarrass you with all this now. Let's simply enjoy this delicious food, maybe even get a little drunk and see what tomorrow brings.'

After dinner they put on some tapes. Ross knew what Tom had better than she did. 'Well, I taped many of his records for him before I left for Australia, and he bought a tape recorder so he could listen to his music without having to keep changing the record. He liked the thirties and forties dance music so I know there's lots of Victor Sylvester, Joe Loss, Glen Miller and the like. Each song seemed to spark a story about his youth and he told me many tales about those days.'

Together they looked through the tapes, which were neatly labelled and in alphabetical order. Ross selected one, plugged the machine in and the dreamy music of Victor Sylvester filled the room.

'May I have the pleasure of the next dance,' he said, taking her in his arms. Afterwards he turned the sound very low and they sat together on the settee and talked. When he put his arm across her shoulders she involuntarily snuggled closer but when his other hand touched her breast she moved, in spite of her longing for the sensation never to end.

'Sorry,' he said, 'let's have a last waltz before I leave, shall we?'

The fact that the music had long ago stopped playing made no difference to either of them as he took her in his arms. He began to sing softly 'Dancing Cheek To Cheek' as he matched his actions to the words, then he kissed her, gently and lingeringly, in complete contrast to the last time, that day in the kitchen when she had told him she was going to marry Nick.

Lying sleepless in bed later she knew she still loved him as much as she ever had. He was the reason she would not commit herself to anyone else, even now, all these years on. Yet nothing could come of it, there were Jane and Nick. Without Nick, whether I marry him or not, I won't be able to keep the manor, she thought, and although Ross isn't living with Jane she is obviously his girlfriend. She fiddled with the little silver friendship ring Ross had bought her on a day out when she was sixteen. The die was cast so many years ago, she thought, and it would never fade, simply imbed itself deeper and deeper.

Chapter 6

The following morning Ross telephoned while she was eating breakfast. 'I have to be out for most of the day, Maura, but how about you coming over to Primrose Cottage around seven for supper. I'll invite Jane too – it will be a chance for you to get to know each other. She's lived in Australia for some years but she is English, from–'

'Sorry, Ross, I've something on this evening. In fact this is really a working trip for me and I'm busy most of the time.'

'That's a pity,' he said quietly, 'because I could have sworn that you enjoyed last evening almost as much as I did. No matter, there'll be other times. Don't work too hard, will you?'

Tears weren't far away when she replaced the phone and she mentally chided herself for minding so much. Introduce her to Jane indeed! Let them have a cosy tête-à-tête, she didn't care. Straightening her shoulders she was determined to get on with the work in hand and put Ross completely out of her mind. She certainly did not intend to be a diversion for him. In any case there was Nick to consider. Although she had refused his ring, they were what she believed the media these days called, 'an item', and she supposed that, even if they never married they were going to be business partners. It seemed that Ross and Jane were the same.

It was two days later when she saw Jane. She had spent most of the day in various departments of the council offices in Trowbridge and had stopped to do some shopping in Salisbury on the way home. Jane was coming through the door of Mothercare.

'Hullo,' she said, 'it's Maura, isn't it?'

Close to she was obviously slightly older than Maura had realized, possibly in her early thirties.

'That's right. And you are Ross's friend, Jane.' Now what on earth had made her say that. Why hadn't she simply said 'and you are Jane?' Jane however didn't seem to find it odd. She smiled warmly at Maura. 'He's a wonderful man, isn't he?' she said. 'Been a real good friend to me. Do you fancy a cup of tea or something?'

It seemed churlish to refuse and ten minutes later they were sitting in a teashop together. Jane said she originally came from

Surrey but only had a distant cousin there now. 'I have been in touch with her and am going to see her while I'm here, but I love Picton and being so near Salisbury. It's a grand city.'

They parted outside the café, Jane to finish her shopping and Maura to go the car park. In spite of not wanting to like her, Maura thought that in other circumstances she could have been friends with Jane. Why did all this have to happen now? What was in Uncle Tom's mind when he left me the manor? Perhaps he thought I would come back here to live – maybe he realized more than I did how much of a country girl I am at heart. She unlocked her car and tried to shake off her despondent feelings. After all, there was a lot of work to be done and although the idea of turning the manor into an upmarket restaurant meant she would be able to keep it and live there again, she couldn't do it without using Nick's money.

She turned into the drive and parked the car. Ross was in the kitchen, a mug of tea in his hand.

'I didn't see your car,' she said.

'I walked. Thought it would do me good. That's a hired car anyway. Might have been cheaper to have bought a little banger to use while I'm here and sold it afterwards.'

'Afterwards?' She tried to make it sound casual, 'You mean when you go back to Australia?'

'Mmm. If I do.'

'I saw your friend Jane in Salisbury,' she said, watching his face.

'Did you? She told me she wanted to do some shopping. I offered to drive her in but she said she'd feel inhibited by having me hanging around and she wanted to browse so she went in on the bus.'

The telephone rang. She called out, 'I'll get it, Mrs Duffy,' and hurried from the room.

It was Nick. 'A quickie, my love, to tell you I'll be down this evening to see how things are going. Everything all right?'

'Fine, Nick. What sort of time. I'll see there's a meal for you.'

'No, don't bother. We'll go into Salisbury to eat. Suss out the competition. See you later, darling.'

She hurried back into the kitchen. 'Do you know where Mrs Duffy is, Ross?'

'In the garden I believe, gathering herbs or something.'

As she moved towards the door he swiftly followed and touched her arm, 'Hey, what's the hurry? I wanted to talk to you, Maura.'

'Sorry, not now. I've things to do.'

'That was your boyfriend on the phone, wasn't it? Is he coming down to check on you, then?'

'Don't be ridiculous,' she said as she moved away. 'Nick and I don't check on each other.'

Ross was still in the kitchen when she returned from finding the housekeeper and telling her they would not need a meal this evening.

'Look, Ross,' she said as quietly as her pounding heart would allow, 'I don't know why you're hanging about. I've told you I'm busy and – and also committed,' she added turning away so she wouldn't have to look into his eyes.

'Me too.' His voice was as soft as velvet. 'Totally committed and have been ever since the night of your seventeenth birthday. I thought you would get the big city thing out of your system after a few months but I was wrong, so wrong. I should have known with your determination you wouldn't be back so soon, but even I never thought it would be five years. In any case I couldn't have offered you anything myself then, but now I can. Maura...' in one stride he was beside her. As his arms closed around her she felt the rush of tears and no amount of swallowing and blinking would stop them. Pressing her tenderly against his chest he murmured, 'There, there, it's all right, Maura, everything will be all right.' It was lovely to feel so warm and loved and for a few moments she gave herself over completely to her feelings, but as the tears abated she pulled away from him. 'This is ridiculous,' she said, feeling a little drunk with emotion.

'Doesn't feel ridiculous to me. In fact it feels exactly right.' His lips softly brushed against her still wet cheeks, 'Maura, my darling, I've waited so long and I love you so much.'

With a great effort she said, 'What about Jane?'

'Jane? I'm not in love with Jane. She's a friend from Australia. Purely platonic.' He kissed her passionately and as they drew apart he said, 'I could say what about Nick to you, but I won't ask such a silly question.'

She moved away slightly, 'What's silly about it? I've been with him four years.'

'You aren't in love with him, that's what's wrong with it.'

'I suppose you think I'm still holding a torch for you. You really are the most conceited person I've ever known, Ross. Now if

94

you'll excuse me I have things to see to.'

'That's OK. Don't mind me. I'll sit and enjoy watching you and if there's any little job I can do just say the word.'

She felt so angry with him. It was almost as though she was seventeen again with all the uncertainties of her emotions running wild. At the door she took a deep breath, turned back to face him and said, 'Just go home and stop causing trouble.' She ran upstairs and threw herself on to the bed. Her tears flowed fast and hot and in the privacy of her old room she didn't try to stop them.

'You're very subdued this evening, Maura,' Nick said when they were ensconced in a restaurant in the heart of Salisbury. 'Everything going according to plan, isn't it? No real problems with the authorities except how slow they are, is there?'

She shook her head. 'It's me. Change of use is fine, Nick. It's the lay-out of the restaurant I'm bothered about.'

'Don't worry about that. It'll look great.' They were sitting side by side on plush red seats at a table laid with a brilliant white cloth and set with cutlery that gleamed like silver. He felt for her hand, 'It's because

95

you're still thinking of the manor as a house to live in rather than a restaurant. You're too close to it at present, but once the alterations are under way and you see how the finished place will be you'll love it.' He squeezed her hand, 'Trust me, sweetie, I'll make The Manor the finest and most exclusive–'

Abruptly she pulled her hand from his grip. 'I don't want to lose the library or the rose garden. I think we should begin small.'

'The library is ideal, Maura, surely you must see that. As for the rose garden I can't see what the fuss is about, because there will still be roses there, it will only be used when the weather is warm. And I've been thinking about the summerhouse. A swimming pool will probably have to wait until we're well established but we could put a gazebo there to house small exhibitions. Cookery, art, fashion, and of course it will be tall enough for people to have a view of the surrounding countryside.'

'No,' she said in a whisper. Her emotions were so close to the surface they threatened to overwhelm her. At that moment the waiter brought the first course and it gave her precious moments to recover. When he left them she said, 'We'll talk about it when we get home, Nick. This looks delectable.'

She picked up her fork and began to eat.

'As you wish, but you're up and down like a seesaw lately. It's not like you. The sooner we get started on this venture the better.' He turned his attention to the food and as the evening progressed he related humorous incidents that had happened to him and several of their friends during the week she had been away from London. She knew he was trying to lighten her mood but she knew also that there would have to be a show-down when they returned to the manor.

Yet in the end the row that ensued was not about plans for the Manor Restaurant but about Ross. 'So what's so special about that broken-down old summerhouse?' Nick said. Then, in a gentler tone, 'I can picture you playing there when you were a little girl. I bet it became many different things for you, like my den in the bushes at the bottom of our garden. Sometimes it was a boat pushing its way through swamplands, sometimes a hideaway from an enemy army, once it was – hey.' His arm came round her as she turned her face from him and sobbed.

'I'm sorry,' she said wiping her eyes a few moments later.

'It's all right, Maura. Memories have a way of catching you unaware, but we all have to move on and in your mind you'll always have those pictures of the child you were. I can see what a wonderful place it must have been for you then, can picture you walking the length of it pretending you were a model and all the fashionable ladies were sitting on the benches watching you. But you don't need the building now because your dream became the reality.'

She was gazing at him, no longer crying but her face still streaked with tears. 'I won't have it pulled down. You don't need it for the restaurant, it doesn't even show from the house.' Moving away from him she said, 'I'm not sure we ought to be doing this, Nick. It's getting out of hand.'

'I'll say it is. You weren't crying for your lost childhood, were you? So what is it? Is that where you secretly met a lover your uncle didn't know about? All this sentimental twaddle about a place you never went near for years.'

In the silence she glanced at Nick's face and saw realization dawn. 'It's that chap Ross, isn't it? Is that why you left?' Suddenly he was gripping her shoulders, 'Answer me, Maura, because we are in this thing together. It could be so good but I have to know now what the situation between you and that – that man was.'

'Yes, Ross and I went about together for a while but it was years ago. You know that until Uncle Tom died I hadn't been back to the manor. I spent much of my childhood here though, and I have always loved it.'

'Where does Ross fit into all this? Is he married? Was he married then? Is that why you left?'

'No,' she shouted back, 'he wasn't and you *know* why I left. Because Uncle Tom didn't want me to take up a modelling career but to get a job in Salisbury. I've told you all this before. We quarrelled but I did see my uncle although I never came down here.'

'I'm not a fool, Maura. There was more to it than that, wasn't there?'

'Nick, I think we had better forget the idea of a restaurant here. I'll simply sell the place and be done with it.'

'No. It's been good with us for the last four years, hasn't it? I'd like to make it permanent. We fit together, we're the same sort of people.'

'I don't think we are, Nick.'

'Of course we are. Coming back has been traumatic for you and I admit I have probably rushed you over this business. I'm sorry about that, Maura, but you know me – once

I've made up my mind about something I go for it. I only considered the idea of a restaurant here in the first place because you were so reluctant to let it go. But I want to do it for different reasons now I've seen it. The place has wonderful possibilities.'

His arm came round her shoulders but it was more of a comforting than a sexual gesture. 'I'll tell you what we'll do, we'll leave the summerhouse for a bit and concentrate on the restaurant. Not for too long of course, because a pool will be an added incentive for people to come here. Meanwhile we can put on fashion shows in the rose garden in summer, an exhibition in the gazebo, and of course always the finest decor and cuisine in the restaurant. But for the moment we'll concentrate on the main part of the house. Once you see how good it's going to be you'll be the one leading the way for other expansions, I know.'

Maura slept very little that night and went down to breakfast with tired eyes and a worried heart. Now that she was back in Picton she knew this was where she wanted to be. She loved the place and with Nick's idea of turning it into a restaurant it could become reality. She could come home.

Although she enjoyed modelling tremendously her career in that direction wasn't going to go on for ever, and she could get to London easily enough from here. Still take modelling jobs if they were offered, but ease off from it gradually. She had fulfilled her dream now. And although I still enjoy the life, she thought, Uncle Tom was right about it not being the glamour job my very young self thought it might turn out to be.

They were all wrong about her happiness in the job, though, because she had relished almost every moment. If Uncle Tom hadn't died she thought she would probably have looked for a change of direction within two or three years anyway. There was always the risk that the modelling agency would have dispensed with her services before then too. It was, as he had said, and she had come to realize, a precarious business. So far she had been fortunate. She wasn't a household name but she made an extremely good living. Yet she didn't have enough money behind her to transform the manor house into an upmarket restaurant. Nick did. She needed his input on the business side of it as well as the extra cash, but was that too high a price to pay?

When the idea was first mooted she visualized it as a small but exclusive place which used the dining room and drawing room but left the library and everything else as it was.

Nick sat down opposite her. 'When is your next assignment, Maura?'

'Day after tomorrow.' She was glad he hadn't started to talk about the plans for the manor yet. First thing in the morning was not her best time of day and although she wasn't usually a bursting into tears kind of person, these last weeks had changed that. She hadn't shed so many since leaving Picton and Ross ... no, she mustn't even think about him – it was far too complicated just now.

'I shall go back tonight or very early tomorrow morning,' Nick said, gazing at her across the plate of eggs and bacon that Mrs Duffy had put in front of him. 'There is a lot to see to with three restaurants. I need to keep my eye on things and without you there this week it hasn't been easy. See if you can clear up the rest of the details before you return, darling, and I promise you that you'll feel better about the alterations once we are under way. It's always the contemplation of change that is the most unsettling but once it's happening you'll feel the excitement too. And when you see the finished project you'll like it, I know.'

He reached across the table to her and patted her hand, 'I do love you, Maura, and I'm looking forward to this joint enterprise. It will be the jewel in Nicholas Page Enterprises and you'll be the pivot, the heart of the best restaurant for miles around. But best of all, it will be here in your own home.'

Chapter 7

Top model, Esmeralda hurt in car crash. Maura paused at the entrance to the tube station when she saw the billboard by the newsvendor. She bought a paper, then hurried into the station.

There wasn't much, just a small paragraph headed by an even smaller photograph of the glamorous model known as Esmeralda. It simply stated that:

...the model, real name, Peggy Smelt, was stable in hospital after the car she was travelling in was involved in an accident just before eleven o'clock last night.

Maura didn't know Esmeralda well, although

their paths had crossed several times. Today would have been another one of those occasions because Esmeralda was to be the leading model in today's fashion show.

Hurriedly she tucked the newspaper into her bag and joined the throng of people leaving the train at Oxford Circus. Five minutes later she turned the corner and ran up the front steps of a cream-and-coffee four-storeyed building. The shiny brass plaque stated simply *The House of Escudo*.

Craig Escudo was standing just inside the door of the salon and caught her as soon as she stepped into the already crowded room.

'Maura, you will be taking Esmeralda's place today. Hurry along to Dot and familiarize yourself with the costumes, she has them ready.'

Feeling slightly bemused she did as he asked. 'Ah,' Dot said warmly, 'your big chance, Maura. This is Craig's most important show and the collection is superb. I'll show you the running order.' Maura's excitement was mounting as she followed the older woman.

'Why me, Dot?'

Dot's answer deflated her a bit, however. 'Same size, Maura.'

'Oh.'

'And Craig knows you will carry it off perfectly.'

This obvious afterthought did little for Maura's confidence and the butterflies started up in her stomach. Esmeralda had been designer Craig Escudo's star for the last two and a half years. Determinedly Maura took a couple of deep breaths. She was good at her job and although Esmeralda was a familiar face at Craig's fashion shows Maura remembered reading somewhere that a model was there to display and sell clothes, not for personal recognition. She had heard on the grapevine that Esmeralda entertained ideas of a film career, so if she did well today who knew what could happen? She might become the top model here. Stranger things had been known. You only had to look at Twiggy to see how far a modelling career could take you. Twiggy's face had gazed out from the cover of one of the collection of vintage Vogue magazines she had by her bed at home now. Not that Maura had dreams of the stage, but...

'Do you know how badly hurt Esmeralda is, Dot?' she asked.

'No, I don't, Maura. Now let's concentrate on this show, shall we?' She walked over to the rail of gowns already in order, waiting for Esmeralda. Lined up on a shelf close by were the accessories to wear with each one, and, again in order, the shoes neatly ranged beneath. Looking at them for a few seconds before she obeyed Dot's imperious look, Maura shivered. For today she really would be in someone else's shoes. Depending on the extent of her injuries this accident could mean the end of Esmeralda's modelling days, she thought. She knew nothing of the other girl's circumstances, but she offered a silent prayer that Esmeralda would recover fully.

Meanwhile it was a wonderful opportunity for her to break out of the ranks and finish her own modelling career on a high note.

The salon was packed and Maura recognized several well-known faces. She didn't feel comfortable in one or two of the creations, but most of them she knew suited both her face and figure and when that happened it was easy to exude enormous confidence.

It was a busy afternoon and when it was finished Craig came over and, putting an arm round her, said quietly, 'Well done, Maura. I'm impressed.'

The following day most of the papers had a picture of her on the catwalk alongside the story of Esmeralda's crash. *Model Maura Lington led the new Escudo Collection with elegance... New face on the fashion scene...*

Nick was delighted. 'This will be good for the opening of the Manor House Restaurant,' he said, hugging her. 'People will come to see you as well as enjoy the cuisine and later we could possibly persuade Escudo to put on a small evening show at the manor.'

'Not so fast, Nick. Nothing is settled yet about the manor as a restaurant. I have many doubts about the whole project.'

'I know, I know, my sweet, but believe me they are all unfounded. I've three very successful eating-houses running already; you've seen how well they do, and in fact you have helped Nick's Palace enormously to become the "in" place for discerning diners.'

'Do you know something – you're beginning to sound like your own adverts, Nick.'

A spasm of annoyance rippled across his face, but he said, 'Maybe. There's nothing wrong with that, surely? Aren't you proud and pleased at these write-ups?' He indicated the pile of papers strewn about the coffee table in front of them. 'You should be. You did a terrific job at very short notice and it's brought you to the attention of the media. That can't be bad. Come on, Maura, anything which enhances business is good and this show has class, just like the Manor House Restaurant will have.'

'Craig Escudo has told me not to talk to reporters nor pose for pictures but to let my agent handle it.'

'He's simply going to be selective Maura and I don't blame him. He doesn't want you caught looking like you've just got out of bed or in less than wholesome surroundings. It's early days yet, but your rate will go up handsomely I hope.'

Maura hadn't thought about that side of things but a wave of delight shot through her when she realized that if she could follow this up in a big way within a year or two she might have enough to finance the manor herself. 'Only I can't afford to wait a year or two,' she murmured.

'What did you say?'

'Oh, nothing really. I was sort of thinking aloud, Nick.'

It was as Nick said. The radio and TV wanted interviews, all the newspapers clamoured for photos and her life story. But she stuck to what she had been told to do and smiled sweetly at them (if they got as far as her) and referred them to her agent.

She gave one short interview to a Sunday

paper, 'I was just doing my job,' she told them. The remark was quoted in various guises in several other papers. *Model in line for stardom says coyly, 'I was only doing my job.'*

Fresh face for The House of Escudo, Maureen Lington, says anyone could have taken over, she was simply the lucky one chosen.

'I didn't say any of the things they've attributed to me,' she moaned to Nick, 'and they've got my name wrong too. Most of them printed my name as Maureen or Moira, yet I spelt it out to them. One even called me Mauverneen.'

Nick chuckled, 'I shouldn't worry. It's getting your name known even if it is the wrong name. You are now firmly associated with The House of Escudo, and not simply as an anonymous model from ... see what I mean?'

'Yes, of course I do, but it's so stupid and I'm not at all sure that I like my name and picture splashed across the pages of some of the papers.'

'It's a brief fame, darling, but one we can cash in on when we open the restaurant. It will ensure the press are there.'

Chapter 8

'Hey, Ross, look at this.' Jane waved the newspaper at him when he came into the kitchen. 'Your lovely girlfriend's made it big with the Escudo Collection.' Folding the paper to the appropriate place, she thrust it under his nose.

Ross read silently. 'Good for Maura,' he said quietly when he looked up from the page. 'She deserves it.'

Jane put a large mug of tea in front of him. 'Want some cake? I made a couple of large fruit ones this morning.'

'Thanks. I shall miss your home cooking when you go back,' he said.

'Marry Maura and you'll be fine. If she can't make cakes, although I bet she can, then her Mrs Duffy will.'

'Even I wouldn't marry someone to get a square meal, Jane.'

'I know, but you would marry the girl you love, whether she could cook or not, wouldn't you?' Without waiting for him to reply she went on, 'People do say those on the outside see more of the game and from my position I can see the whole field. You need to get in there and ask her and to tell her why you haven't done so before. I'm being serious now, Ross.'

He turned away. 'Easier said than done, Jane. In the time we've been apart she's led a very different sort of life. And now,' he tapped the newspaper, 'she'll be more reluctant than ever to give it up and become a farmer's wife.'

'Are you going to ring and congratulate her?' She cut a sizable piece from the golden-brown cake, put it on a plate and laid it in front of him.

'Thanks.' He reached for the paper and read the interview again. 'I don't think so, Jane,' he said.

Later, out in the fields, his thoughts returned to the piece and he imagined Maura reading it. How was she feeling? Excited? Thrilled? Recalling her words about her career from a few weeks back when she had said that one place was very like another in her travelling to exotic locations because of her work, he wondered. She had made it clear that she loved her job, yet she was ready to come back and settle in the manor if she could afford to.

He gazed over his land, visualizing it in a few months' time, vibrant with crops, then went on towards the fence on the far side. The two new panels were lying on the perimeter ready to be installed when he had taken the remains of the rotting broken ones out. As he worked he wondered if it was time for him to cut out the old in his life too.

He admitted to himself that at first when Maura went off to London he visited her uncle mostly so that he could have news of her. It wasn't long, though, before he grew to like Tom Wareham and enjoy his company anyway. It was Tom who taught him the rudiments of chess and mah-jong, and always during the times he spent with the older man they talked about Maura. Of course, Tom wouldn't have known much about her social life and of her liaison with that restaurateur, but...

'Blast,' he shouted aloud as the hammer slipped and fell to the ground. He danced around nursing his rapidly swelling thumb for a few moments, then bent to retrieve the tool and continue.

'Am I beating my head against an unbeatable fence,' he wondered aloud, secure in the knowledge that he was far enough away from humanity down here not to be overheard.

'I love her so much and she loved me once. She surely doesn't love that stuck-up prig she brought down here. Her responses to me prove that. Yet she has stayed with him for four years and Maura's never been the sort of girl to do anything she didn't want to.'

'If – if she and I did marry now, would she one day blame me for stopping her career?' He banged the nails in with such force, taking his frustrations out on the work he was doing. After all, he thought, things are really opening up for her now. She's obviously done pretty well, but this is like a second coming. Models were becoming famous in their own right...

Wearily he put down his hammer for a moment and rubbed his hand across his eyes. His thumb began to throb but he intended to finish the job before going back to the farmhouse.

Material things were coming together for him too now, and for the first time in his life he was in a position to offer her a decent living. Yet it looked as if that bumptious man she was going about with had his feet firmly under the table. Although she said she was going to marry him, this Nicholas Page, there was no ring on her finger yet. Suddenly he chuckled aloud. *'All's fair in love and war,* they say, so until the day she tells me they've set a date for the wedding I'll stake my claim.'

With renewed vigour he returned to the fence. When it was finished he stood for a moment, checking that it was OK, then gathered his tools together and trudged back to the farmhouse.

Now the thumb was showing a nasty bruise – what his grandmother used to call a devil's pinch, with the blood beneath the skin. He smiled to himself as he recalled how scared he'd felt the first time she said it to him. He had woken up in the middle of the night screaming that the devil was there trying to get him out of bed. His mother had comforted him and his gran had assured him that a devil's pinch was simply a silly name for the type of injury he had sustained. He smiled at the childhood memory as he poured a drop of disinfectant into a small bowl and soaked his hand which was aching pretty badly. No point in taking chances because he couldn't afford to be incapacitated. Not with the plans he had for the land.

Later that evening he decided he would take Jane's advice and telephone Maura to congratulate her. Jane had retired to her room saying she had some letters to write.

He dialled the number dear old Tom had given him long ago and which he had never before used.

A man's voice answered. Nicholas bloody Page.

'Who was that on the phone, Nick?' Maura came from the shower, a pretty blue bath-robe wrapped around her slender figure.

'Don't know. Wrong number probably. As soon as I answered whoever it was put the phone down.'

It rang again at that moment and Maura picked up the receiver. It was someone wanting her for a modelling job. She referred them to her agent.

'I shall have to change this number or go ex-directory,' she said. 'It's hardly stopped ringing since those reports in the paper. That's good, of course, and I'm not complaining, but I don't keep the diary – my agent does.' She ran into the bedroom to get changed and heard it ring again.

'Another potential booking,' Nick said when she returned. 'I put him on to your agent, but this couldn't have come at a better time, Maura. It practically guarantees success for the opening. Your name will draw people in and when they've been once the food, decor and ambiance of the place will bring them back.'

'Nothing is settled yet, Nick, I have reservations ...'

He laughed loudly, 'So will they, our prospective diners. They'll be queuing up to book a table, so it's more important than ever that we sort this deal out as fast as possible now. Strike while everything is bubbling.'

Chapter 9

The following day Maura's agent rang with a list of bookings. 'By the way,' he said, 'someone called Jim Wareham rang. Said he was your cousin and had been trying to find you. Said he saw your write-ups in the papers and wanted to be put in touch.'

'Did you give him my address?'

'Of course not. You get these people who jump on the bandwagon when they think there might be something in it for them. Happens all the time when you get your name in the papers. But I thought I'd better warn you, in case he tries to get into one of your sessions.'

'Actually,' she said, 'he could be genuine because I do have a cousin called Jim Wareham, but I haven't seen him for years.'

'Well, in that case it's up to you, of course. My advice would be to ignore it. I expect he's after money and maybe even fame, that's usually the way of it when long-lost people turn up out of the blue. Opportunists mostly.'

'Well, yes,' she said. 'Maybe if he telephones again you could get *his* number, then I can ring him if I think I should. It's true that we did lose touch, though.'

'OK, Maura. Will do.'

She wondered if that was who had rung the flat last night when she was changing and Nick had answered. Then she dismissed the idea. If it had been Jim then he would have got her number from the directory and wouldn't have needed to ring her agent for it.

She had this crazy idea in her head that it had been Ross last night because Nick had said no one answered and the phone was put down. It was the sort of action he'd take, she thought, because he would recognize Nick's voice. He wouldn't be ringing to 'jump on the bandwagon' as the agent suggested though.

117

With all the work coming in she couldn't see when she would be able to get down to Picton again. Her normal work, a lot of it with Escudo now, would keep her in town for a couple more days at least but maybe at the weekend she could make it. On impulse she rang her agent back and asked him not to book her for every day but to always leave either Mondays or Fridays clear, preferably both. That should give her an opportunity for some long weekends at the manor to sort out her affairs and decide just what she was going to do with her inheritance before all the permissions and plans for change of use were approved.

He reluctantly agreed to do this. 'But you need to be available now to the highest bidder,' he said. 'You–'

'Highest bidder! I'm not a commodity, I'm a person,' she told him angrily, 'and if someone is really keen they will fit in with my plans.'

'Very well, but remember that although you are a bit of a sensation right now, you aren't the face of any famous house or product yet and are not in a position to dictate terms.'

It was a sobering thought. Once, five, four, even only two or three years ago this was what she had wanted more than anything else. Now – well, she thought, I love modelling, but it isn't the high spot of my life any more. I wonder if it ever has been?

'Yes,' she said, thinking aloud. 'I was young and ambitious and I needed to prove myself. I've done that now and in this business, like it is with certain sports, it is a young person's world. I'm still of an age to go on modelling for at least another four or five years, and possibly beyond if I look after myself and if I really want to, but do I want to? I'm not one hundred per cent certain about that now.'

She realized that being left the manor house by Uncle Tom had focused her mind sharply. The place was too large for her alone and in any case she needed to earn a living. The other side of her argument with herself was that she had adored living in London and being part of the modelling world, but she was ready to move on. Nicholas Page had the vision to see how she could have the best of both worlds. Keep the manor house yet still have a career and a business. With his money and her property she knew it could work, a beautiful restaurant and being back in the country which she now knew was her spiritual home. She needed to stay strong about too many changes to the manor, though, and back here, away from the pressures of both Nicholas and Ross she felt confident she could do it.

It had seemed so simple, she thought, but now there are these other elements creeping in. No, they've been there all the time really. My reluctance to commit to a lifetime with Nick and my love for Ross which has never gone away. I've just buried them beneath a busy life. Whatever Ross does, stay in England or return to Australia, it isn't going to make any difference to my feelings, only what I do about them. If he stays here it would be better for me to make a clean break, sell the manor and stay in London. If he goes to Oz I could run the manor as a restaurant with Nick as a business partner.

Maura had gone to the hospital to see Esmeralda and knew that it would be many weeks, maybe even months, before the girl was fit enough to consider a return to her modelling career.

'By that time everyone will have forgotten me,' Esmeralda said. 'I'll be an also-ran. I'm lucky my face wasn't injured; the scars on my body will heal but doctors here have told me that there could be a weakness in my ankles which I'll need to be careful about. I shall also need intensive physiotherapy they said, so...'

She brushed her hand over her eyes. 'Lucky to be alive really, and it gave you your chance. I'd have fought tooth and nail to stay the lead model if fate hadn't taken a hand like this – believe me you wouldn't have had a look-in if there had been any way I could have still done the job. As it is I've been thinking I may try for an acting career if modelling is out for me in future. It's something I've always wanted to do.'

Maura thought about something else Esmeralda had told her before she left. She thanked her for coming and said that Craig Escudo had not been near. 'I had a card which said something like, *bad luck you missed the big show but all went very well I'm happy to say. Hope you soon feel better.* He'd already written me off, you see. Modelling's a tough way to make a living, Maura, so make the most of it while you can and good luck.'

Chapter 10

Jim Wareham stood on the pavement at the foot of the steps of the Escudo building. He had watched from the corner for several days trying to decide which of the young ladies entering the building was his cousin, Maura. He hadn't seen her since she was a child and the photograph in the paper that had led him to seek her out had been blurred and very small. The larger, clearer one had been of the model Esmeralda, the one injured in a car smash. It was good fortune for him, he thought, that his little cousin was suddenly newsworthy because before that item in the paper his only knowledge of her grown-up life was that she had left the manor to become a model in London.

When he learned of his stepfather's death and the legacy Maura had inherited he knew it was time to come back from Canada. He had planned to go to Picton and see what was happening in the manor house, but had been laid low with a virus for several weeks and had been unable to travel. When he did eventually reach England he rented a room in a lodging house in East London for a month, reasoning that that would give him enough time to stake his claim to the manor.

Although he had been estranged from the family for many years he kept an eye on what was happening to his stepfather through a friend who still lived in England. This man had opted out of the traditional lifestyle of his own family many years ago.

Before Jim went to Canada the two of them had roamed the countryside together, doing odd jobs when there was nothing else and they needed to eat. They were adept at getting a meal in a pub and getting out without paying and as that grew more difficult because most places were taking the money first they worked out other ways of existing, sometimes quite comfortably, without doing much work and without paying for food and services. One of their ploys was to put a card in a newsagent's window offering a magic hour for a very reasonable price. *A fun-filled hour of laughter*, it read, *we do simple tricks, some you will never have seen before. You will be amazed and delighted.*

They always did a couple of genuine tricks to begin with, then came the con. Freddie, who had worked with a magician for a few years in his early career, would ask for a £20, £10 or £5 note from everyone. 'Of course if you only have a fifty that will do,' he would say. The whole lot went into a box which Jim produced from a small old-fashioned-looking suitcase, which was then placed by the door where he was standing. Freddie announced his final piece of magic, 'before we see if we can conjure your money back for you.'

Sometimes he would joke, 'We only lost it once when a money-eating mouse gnawed through the case and chewed the notes up.' He would then pull a toy mouse from his pocket and say, 'Won't happen today, Ferdinand is in here so your money is safe.' Then straight into his final trick while they were still laughing.

The dodgy part of this was not knowing the denomination of the notes beforehand but Jim always carried a small notebook. 'To make sure my partner doesn't pocket it and you get it all back eventually,' he would joke, 'I shall write it in the magic book.' Which he did. Four fivers, eight tenners, three twenties or whatever the ratio on that day was. 'Like us, money needs company,' Freddie would say, 'the more in the box the faster it will disappear and the more impressive the result will be.' Usually everyone dug into their wallets and purses. The box went into the case which had a false floor triggered by the locking device as Jim closed it. Jim would put the case on the floor next to him and make circular movements over it, then a zooming movement towards his partner to indicate that the money was moving towards him.

Freddie's stage jacket had many inside pockets, each filled with counterfeit notes, even one at the top containing a few fifties although they had never needed them. While the audience was applauding the last trick Freddie would say, 'Open the box, Jim,' which he did with a flourish to show an empty box. Freddie would put his hand into his jacket pockets and produce the notes. Jim, once more consulting his notebook, would read out the relevant quantities as Freddie handed the money over. They took a bow, Jim picked up the suitcase and the rest of their props and took them outside to the car while Freddie collected their payment cheque. They always pleasantly refused to stay for a meal or a drink or anything because of another engagement within the hour. The counterfeit notes were excellent and it was often weeks or months before one was discovered when proffered for payment somewhere. It would be very difficult to prove where it had come from even if anyone suspected.

That had been a good con, Jim reflected, usually netting between £100 to £200 as well as their fee, and even more at really large gatherings. Not bad for an hour's work. It only stopped when Freddie had to go into hospital for several months.

Jim wore lovat-green trousers and a blazer, the only smart clothes he possessed, while loitering around the building where Maura worked. He hoped to be able to see her without going in and making himself known to whoever was in charge because if Maura refused to see him and he was thrown out, his face would be known to them all and his chance of speaking to her gone. He had decided to take the reasonable approach and talk about reconciliation with his stepfather just a week or so before he died. And about a promise from the old man that he would now reinstate him in his will, but of course, there hadn't been time. He would say that had that happened he would, of course, have shared the money from the sale of the manor with Maura; it would be the only fair thing to do as they obviously both had a claim. Once he had a foot in the door he could work out how to get the entire estate. He might even have to marry his cousin to do that, but he saw no problem there, unless she was already married.

He spotted a young lady heading for the building. 'Excuse me,' he said, 'I'm looking for my cousin who is a model here. I've just returned to the old country from Canada and I came over without her address. I haven't seen her since she was a small girl and I have some important news for her. Her name is Maura.' The young woman returned his smile, but continued up the steps. 'I'm sorry I can't help you,' she said.

He tried the same approach with the next two who entered the building, but they had obviously all been warned not to talk to anyone. Probably in case any enquirers were the press in disguise, since they also murmured some platitude and hurried on. Ridiculous the way they shielded these fashion garments as though they were vitally important secrets until they were ready to show them, he thought. He moved away and round the corner. Didn't want the management coming out and having him for harassment of their girls. Perhaps the best thing would be to write to Maura. He thought about this for a few moments before ditching the idea. If she didn't reply he was cut off anyway and he needed to keep his options open. He could go down to the manor but there was no guarantee she would be there either. Maybe a short note addressed to her and handed in here would do it. They would surely have to give it to her and she might be intrigued enough to meet him. He had checked the telephone directory for her number and although it was listed he couldn't get through. 'This number has been changed,' he was told, 'and the new one is ex-directory, I'm afraid.' So that route was out.

Jim tried to remember what Maura had looked like as a child – whether she had any distinguishing marks, but he didn't think so. He had never taken a great deal of notice of the child, yet here she was now, the owner of a property that would fetch a tidy sum if he wasn't mistaken. Totally unfair – he was the old man's stepson after all, and this girl was simply his niece.

After another quarter of an hour he gave up. He would have to find another way to contact her. What was it his mother used to say? *There is more than one way to kill a cat.* Right, he thought, there is also more than one way to inherit a fortune, because there must have been some money with the property too. As he moved from the corner to the front of the building, intending to walk past and towards the tube station, he had his slice of luck. A red car pulled up and a young lady alighted. She blew a kiss to the driver, 'Thanks, Nick,' she said, then walked up the steps and disappeared inside the building. Instinctively Jim knew he had found Maura. He looked at the number as the car pulled away and hoped he could remember it because he had nothing on him with which to write it down. The girl's face, though, was a pretty picture in his mind. All he had to do was to try to talk to her when she came out, or, failing that, jump into a cab and follow the car if the same one came to collect her later.

Smiling happily to himself he walked along the road in search of a place to buy a cup of tea. He didn't know how long she would be there; in fact, he thought quite cheerily, I don't know anything about the fashion and model world, but I daresay she'll be an hour or so. He returned to the corner forty-five minutes later and waited and watched. His instinct told him this was Maura, the woman he was seeking, and he went over in his mind the story he was going to pitch to her. She was only a child at the time he left the family and he doubted if she knew much of the story. In any case, he thought now, she would have their version of it and he intended to offer his. And he'd make her believe it.

He had to wait twenty minutes more. He walked a little way down the street, but was afraid to go too far in case she came out and was whisked away, yet he didn't want to look suspicious by standing right outside the building for any length of time. The car she had arrived in did not return to collect her. She came down the steps chatting with another girl and they set off walking quite quickly in the direction of Oxford Circus tube station. Jim followed. It was easy enough to get up close and hear which zone she bought a ticket for. Jim bought one for the same journey as Maura, for he was certain it was her, and her friend had done. The friend reached her destination first which made it very easy for him to follow Maura on to the platform when she alighted at Finsbury Park and accidentally bump into her as they both hurried for the exit.

He had his story ready, one he had improvised during the short tube-train journey.

130

'I'm so sorry,' he said softly, 'I'm always being told off for rushing everywhere. I haven't hurt you, have I?'

'Not at all.' She smiled at him. 'You go first, I'm not in a hurry this evening.'

'Thank you.' He had intended to follow her but the tables had been turned so he went on a few steps, then stopped suddenly and wheeled round to face her. 'I knew I'd seen you before,' he said. 'You look exactly like a cousin of mine. Well, I say *seen*, but in photographs only, because I've been living abroad for years, but my stepfather used to keep me up to date on family news. I haven't actually *seen* Maura in the flesh so to speak, since she was a very small child, but he used to send me pictures from time to time. He was very proud of her – told me she had grown into such a beautiful young lady. I'm on my way to visit her now, actually. If I may say so, you are the image of a picture he sent me shortly before he died a few months ago. You couldn't be – no of course not. Different hairstyle but so, so similar. They do say we all have a double, don't they? Goodnight, miss. Have a great evening.' He moved on and had emerged from the underground station when her voice just behind him said, 'Did you say your cousin's name was Maura?'

Turning to look at her once more he said, 'Yes, that's right, Maura. It's a pretty name, isn't it?' He paused for just a couple of seconds. He was so carried away with his act that if he had been wearing a hat he would have raised it to her. Instead he said 'Don't tell me you know her, that would be too much.'

'I not only know her, I am Maura,' she said. 'You must be Jim?'

'By all that's wonderful!' He looked suitably amazed. 'Maura, cousin Maura.' He held out his hand. 'Tom gave me your address and phone number last time I was over but I had to get back and I promised myself I would look you up on my next visit. I tried to ring you but they said the number had been changed and was now ex-directory; it's a bit cheeky, I know, but I thought I would call just on the off-chance.' A happy smile spread across his face. 'I can't believe I'm actually talking to Aunt Lucy's daughter. You were just a tiny child when I saw you last.'

She took him to her flat and as they went in he slapped his hand against his face, 'I was going to buy you some flowers on the way here,' he said. 'You know, arriving out of the blue like this, but I was so thrilled to find you it went out of my head. I'll get you some next time.'

'Oh Jim, there's no need. It is good to catch up with some of the family. Tell me, when did you last see Uncle Tom?'

'A few months before he died, Maura. I was over on business, a flying visit, but I made sure I saw him because we had years of estrangement, as you probably know. We only really got together again last year – a family row which I won't go into now, but misunderstandings all round as these things so often are. We had been so close once and it hurt me terribly when, through no fault of my own, I was not welcome any longer.'

Maura said quietly, 'He was a good man. I had my differences with him too, but he looked after me so well and I sometimes feel guilty that I didn't let him know how much he meant to me more often. I got caught up in a busy life and didn't see him as often as I should have, or even as much as I would have liked to.'

Jim couldn't believe his good fortune at her words. 'I'm sure he knew how you appreciated him, Maura. For my part I am so relieved that he and I made up our quarrel last year and got ourselves back to a proper father and son relationship. We talked for a long while on that last visit and he told me that he was going to change his will, but that he wanted me to make sure that you were well looked after.'

Maura looked hard at this man, her cousin, and a warning bell seemed to ring inside her head. 'I didn't know you had seen him last year, Jim. He never mentioned it to me and he always took me to lunch or came here to the flat when he was in town.'

'I don't suppose he thought you'd be interested – after all, you hardly knew me, did you? Whereas he had helped to bring me up. Anyway, it's all water under the bridge now, isn't it, because I gather he left you the manor. Didn't have time to get the new will approved and official, I guess, so I lost out. It's probably lying around the manor somewhere because he had it all down on a foolscap pad which he planned to take to his solicitor. He showed it to me. He'd left you a sizable sum, as I recall.'

Stunned, Maura said quietly, 'It seems strange to me that he told you all this because until he died I had no idea he was going to leave me his home.'

The doorbell rang. Maura rose to answer it. She knew it would be Nick. He had got his own key and she had one to his flat above the restaurant in the West End. He often forgot his.

Jim frowned when he heard a man's voice. It had all been going so well, but he really didn't want a boyfriend on the scene. It could make life difficult. He stood up as Maura returned, followed by Nick.

'Nick, this is my cousin Jim from Canada. Jim, this is Nicholas Page,' she said.

Chapter 11

Jim didn't stay long after Nick arrived. Long enough to discover that he owned three restaurants in London and was very much at home in his cousin's flat.

'You're a lucky man,' he said. 'It's always been my dream to own a restaurant and cook fab food for people.'

'Can you cook? Are you any good at it?' Nick flashed questions at him but Jim answered calmly enough.

'Oh yes. I've worked as a chef in a couple of the finest hotels in Canada. I like moving on, though. Never been one to stay in the same place for too long.'

'And you're Tom Wareham's stepson, I understand.'

'That's right. Good guy was Tom.'

'Same name. Did he adopt you?'

'No. I was known by his name because he married my mother but my real dad wouldn't agree to an adoption although Tom wanted to. Make it all legal you know. But that's only a formality. We were father and son in all the things that mattered.'

'I thought your mother was a widow,' Maura said quietly.

'She was latterly, but not when she first got together with Tom. The old man had left her, so I was very happy to take my step-father's name. He wanted to adopt me when she divorced my father but they were both rather slack about signing papers, I'm afraid.' He laughed indulgently. 'It didn't matter, really, Tom couldn't have treated me better, and to all intents and purposes I was his son. Of course if he had made it legal I would have inherited instead of you, cuz.' He turned to Maura and smiled at her. 'That would have curbed my wanderings, wouldn't it?' There was a brief silence, then Jim went on, 'Still, it's good that the manor has stayed in the family and not gone to strangers. I must pop down and see it again while I'm over here.'

When neither Maura nor Nick took that remark further he stood up. 'Must get going. I came on the off-chance to make contact now that I'm over here for a few months, Maura. Tom was right, you are a stunning girl. We must keep in touch, guardians of the family home and all that, y'know.' As he moved towards the door he said, 'Oh, jot your telephone number down will you, love? Then I can come over when you haven't any plans and we can catch up with things.' Turning to Nick he held out his hand. 'Good to meet you, Nicholas, must call in to one of your eating-houses for a meal sometime. Where are they?'

'All in London. Nick's Café's in Mile End Road, Nick's Place is in Leyton and Nick's Palace is in Oxford Street in the West End. We cater for all levels. The food's good in all of them, just different in style and price.'

Maura gave Jim a card with her name and her agent's telephone number. 'Thanks for seeking me out,' she said. 'I'm rather busy this next few weeks but we can get together again before you go back to Canada, I hope. Now I've taken Esmeralda's place with Escudo life has become doubly busy, but it will settle down soon.' She walked to the front door with him and he kissed her on both cheeks.

'You're my cousin yet I scarcely know you,' he said. 'There's not many of us left so we ought to stick together, don't you think?'

'Yes, of course,' she said quietly as she ushered him through the door.

'You were a bit brisk with him, Nick, weren't you?'

'Possibly, but don't you find it odd that he has turned up now, when you have just inherited a family property?'

'Yes, I rather think I do. I was happy to see him at first because I haven't much family now Uncle Tom's gone, but – well he did seem to be probing and angling for an invitation to the manor, didn't you think?'

'Most definitely. You hadn't seen him for how long?'

'Since I was about four or five. Something like that, I can't remember exactly but I know Uncle Tom and he had a row and that was it. I've no idea what it was all about.'

'He's your uncle's stepson?'

'Yes. I always understood that Uncle Tom married a widow who had a young lad.'

'I don't trust him, Maura. There's something – something shifty about him for all

138

that he was falling over himself to appear pleasant and happy-go-lucky.'

'His attitude seemed to change when you arrived,' she said. 'He was boyish and sort of bubbly before that.'

'Hmm. You didn't give him your telephone number, did you?'

'No, it's my agent's number on the card. He can deal with him. Except, of course, he knows where I live now. Do you suppose he resents me having the manor, Nick? He made that jocular remark about it, didn't he? But underneath he may think he is entitled to it.'

'It was certainly the impression I got, Maura. Neither of us mentioned our plans for it so he obviously thinks you are either going to live there or sell it. Let's forget him for now, darling, and concentrate on how things are going in that direction. Have you heard any more from the planners or solicitors?'

She shook her head. 'But I thought I would try and get down for a day next week if I can. Have to check work schedules, of course, but if I go down late afternoon or early evening I can do some sorting out of personal things. I've more books and ornaments than I realized, and some clothes and shoes stored away in boxes; and of course, there's all of Uncle Tom's stuff. I can check on everything else the following day and be back here in the evening.'

Jim seethed with anger as he walked to the station. A quarter of an hour with her on her own and he felt sure he would have had an invitation to the manor the next time she went down. That stupid berk of a boyfriend had queered his pitch. Changed the direction of the conversation and made her suspicious and cold towards him. Sod it.

He walked fast and furiously and by the time he was sitting on the train he had worked a little of his frustration off. It would simply take longer than he'd expected to sort it out, he thought, which was a damn nuisance because London was expensive and he had very little money. He had a few good clothes, though, enough to bluff his way into places that would not normally be accessible to him.

He had some forged credentials too – a strange smile flickered across his face. The chap Nicholas hadn't believed him when he said he had worked in two of Canada's best hotels, he could tell. He'd have to eat his words if he actually applied for a job with him, maybe for that West End eatery, what was it he called it? Nick's Palace – what a common name for something that he had implied was top drawer.

His thoughts wandered around his cousin and her status. Not yet married, quite a beauty in a fresh sort of way, not over-sophisticated. He could do worse than marry her. Nothing to stop him, really, because there was no blood relationship. Tom was her mother's brother and nothing to do with him. His mother had been an outsider who had simply married into the family. 'It's a thought,' he muttered to himself when he left the train and was walking home along the litter-strewn streets of the East End. How London had deteriorated since he had lived here. A vision of the clean streets of Canada flashed into his mind. He turned into a side street and walked down to the two rooms he was renting. What a comparison after Maura's light and airy flat.

As he changed from his decent trousers and blazer into an old pair of jeans and crumpled T-shirt he wondered how close the relationship between his cousin and Nicholas Page was. She hadn't been wearing an engagement ring, but that didn't necessarily mean that they weren't committed to each other. He had certainly dominated the conversation and Maura had seemed content to let him do so.

He began to fantasize what marriage to Maura could be like. They would have money and if she carried on modelling entry to a world he fancied. Come to think about it, simply living in the manor at Picton would gain him access to places he could enjoy too. She was a looker and he enjoyed women as well as men. In the line of business she was in she would be used to all sorts and might even welcome someone who didn't need her all the time.

Money, a roomy and splendid place to live near a city where the name of Wareham was pretty well respected if things down there hadn't changed too drastically. He could do a lot worse, he reflected.

Of course she might be planning to sell the manor, he hadn't had a chance to find out before that wretched boyfriend arrived. Well, if she was it would give them plenty of cash to buy something else equally agreeable and maybe have money over as well.

As he snuggled down to sleep he thought the day hadn't been a total disaster after all. Better to know what you are up against, then you can plan your strategy, he thought.

Anyway, the boyfriend couldn't be there all the time, not with three restaurants to run. All he had to do was catch her on her own and things he wanted would start happening, he felt sure.

Chapter 12

Maura came down to Salisbury by train because her car packed up the day before and had to go to the garage. She seldom used it for getting to work, unless she was doing outdoor shots on Hampstead Heath or Richmond, a favourite spot for riverside pictures. For anything else she went by bus or tube, usually tube because it was faster.

As she arrived at Salisbury railway station almost the first people she saw were Ross and Jane. They were waiting on the adjoining platform where a train was just arriving. They both waved vigorously and Ross called out, 'I'll give you a lift back, Maura.' He kissed Jane and gave her a big hug, before almost lifting her into the carriage. They seemed to be laughing over her huge haversack, which was hampering them. Then he strode the short distance over to Maura and, as Jane's train moved from the other line, he turned towards it and blew her a kiss.

'This is a bit of luck,' he said to Maura. 'Why didn't you let me know you were coming?'

'I never have before.'

'I thought you usually drove down, anyway.'

'My car's out of action. Only a small job, the garage said. It will be ready when I get back.'

Ross seemed to be in an *I will not let you rile me* mood in spite of her brisk answers. He was smiling as he picked up her case, tucked her arm into his and set off.

She slid her arm away and he let out a theatrical sigh. 'You can't blame me for trying, Maura, but OK, I'll behave. Feeling as I do about you the temptation is sometimes too much, though. When I saw you on the platform it made my day. I wanted to rush over and hug you.'

'You were making a pretty good job of doing that with your girlfriend,' she said.

'Jane isn't my girlfriend, Maura. I'm looking after her while she's in England, that's all there is to it. You're the one I want in that

144

role, as you well know. It doesn't mean I can't kiss an old friend's wife sometimes, though. But you are my world, or rather I would like you to be. I'm fond of Jane, I want her to be happy. I love her as a friend but I'm not in love with her. Can you understand that?'

'No. You were positively fawning over the girl, but she's obviously going away for a few days and I'm here. That makes it very convenient for you, doesn't it? Well, it won't wash with me, Ross. I can get a taxi, don't you bother.'

She snatched her small case from him and ran down the slope from the platform. She was halfway up the one leading to the way out when he caught her.

'You're pretty impressive when you're angry, Maura, but in this instance you have no need to be – angry I mean. I expect Nicholas whatever his name is, kissed you like that before you left. It doesn't have any special meaning. Jane has had a rough time and no way would I abandon her in a strange country. Her husband was a good friend of mine and–'

'I don't care who she is, just let go of me.' She prised his arm from hers with her free hand. The sudden movement on the steep incline caused her to wobble and he grabbed

145

her to prevent her from falling. For a few moments she thought she had ricked her ankle, and she moved it gingerly from side to side. Whew, thank heaven it was a false alarm.

'Is your foot all right,' Ross said, looking down but still holding on to her.

'Of course.' She pulled away from him and transferred the neat navy-blue case into her other hand with such a flourish that her shoulder bag swung back towards him, narrowly missing his face.

'You shouldn't try to run in those ridiculous high heels,' he said, ignoring the incident. 'You've such pretty ankles – made for the catwalk, not for racing up and down slopes.'

'Oh, you're insufferable, Ross Edwards. Just leave me alone, will you?'

'Certainly.' He strode ahead of her and within seconds had reached the top and disappeared from her view. She felt tears gathering in her eyes and blinked them away before she made a fool of herself. As if she hadn't enough to worry about, with the uncertainty of being able to keep her inheritance, the pressure Nick was putting on to have his way with the proposed restaurant, and her cousin's sudden emergence after all the years of silence. The last thing she needed now was the hassle of quarrelling with the one man she had loved since the night of her seventeenth birthday party.

She emerged into the station forecourt and Ross was waiting. Gently but firmly he took the case from her. 'My car is just over here, Maura. It would be rash to take a taxi when I'm going your way, wouldn't it? You have my word that I will drop you at the manor and leave without trying to come inside.'

She felt her mouth curve into a smile in spite of herself, and Ross added very, very softly, 'Unless I am invited in by my passenger, of course. That would be a different matter altogether.' He put her case on the back seat before slipping into the front beside her. 'Do you need to stop off and get anything here first? Milk, bread...?'

She knew he was saying this to make her talk to him, and she couldn't stay cross for long. 'No thank you, Ross. Mrs Duffy will have bought everything we need for the next couple of days.'

'Right, off we go then.' He released the handbrake, slid the car into gear and moved smoothly away from the station and down Fisherton Street. When they entered Picton

Maura felt almost light-headed. She was back, and although there were obviously problems to be solved here, there was a warm, comfortable feeling creeping over her, especially as the little car turned into the drive at the manor.

As Ross handed over her soft-topped case she said quietly, 'You'd better come in for a cuppa, Ross. Mrs Duffy will think it odd if you don't.'

'Well, thank you, I accept. It will save me making one when I get back and of course it will placate Mrs D.' His face seemed to crease into a dozen or so smiles, they were there in his eyes, his lips, his cheeks, even his nose was quivering slightly with mirth and happiness. 'Oh Maura, why do we always quarrel?' he said softly as he followed her through the back door and into the kitchen.

'How long are you here for?' he asked when they were drinking their mugs of tea.

'The rest of today and most of tomorrow. I shall go back late afternoon or early evening because I'm working early the following morning. Not long enough to do all the things I need to but I can make a start.'

He finished his tea and stood up. 'I've a fair bit to see to myself,' he said. 'Land always needs attention, but I'll be free this evening from about seven. Any chance of a meal together? Salisbury, a country pub, your place or mine? After all we both need to eat, don't we?'

He suddenly looked vulnerable, not so much in charge as he had at the station and she couldn't deny to herself how very much she wanted to be with him. Oh, to hell with it, she thought, why not?

'All right. Seven o'clock. You can choose the place, but keep in mind that I haven't any glamour clothes with me this trip. Jeans, a cotton skirt and a couple of very basic tops.'

He did hug her then. 'I'll be here on the dot of seven,' he said, pursing his lips in a make-believe kiss, 'I love you, Maura.' Then he was gone, making Mrs Duffy, who came back into the kitchen a few seconds afterwards say, 'Goodness he was in a hurry, but he looked pretty happy. Grinning like a Cheshire cat he was. I've put your case in your room, miss.'

'Thanks, Mrs D. By the way I'll be eating out this evening.'

Chapter 13

They went to an old coaching inn a few miles from Picton. As they walked across the cobbled yard Ross smiled at her. 'There's a restaurant here in what used to be the stables, and the food is good. A great variety of hot and cold meals. Salads, fish, home-made steak-and-kidney puddings, roasts, cottage pies, that sort of thing. Nothing too way out. They go to town on the desserts though, everything from apple pies and crumbles to fancy concoctions piled with strawberries, raspberries, exotic fruits and topped with ice cream or fresh cream, whichever you prefer. And a whole range in between.'

It was lovely inside, with oak beams criss-crossing its huge length and windows that looked out on to fields where, in the distance, horses grazed.

'I've never been here before,' she said. 'It's like a little piece of old England before everything became so mechanized and fast-moving.'

'It used to be just the pub, but a couple of years ago they turned the old stables into this restaurant.'

Maura gazed round with interest. 'Did they? You know the manor is going to be a restaurant, Ross?'

'No, I didn't know that,' he said quietly. 'A restaurant.' He looked thoughtful. 'Are you happy with that idea?'

Uncanny how he always hit the vital spot. She was silent for several minutes, fussing with her bag and not looking at him. Then he reached across the table and touched her hand. She looked directly at him.

'Not really,' she said in a steady voice, 'but it's the only way I can keep it on at present.'

'I see. Is Nicholas Page going to run it – be a business partner, then? I don't want to pry, but if you want to talk about it I'm a good listener. And sometimes an uninvolved person can see the good and bad points clearly.'

She didn't mean it to, but a great and very deep sigh escaped. 'It's not the ideal situation from my point of view, but it does mean I won't have to sell it. There is a lot of deterioration there, more than I at first thought. While it isn't exactly crumbling to pieces, when you delve into the situation it is in a pretty bad way. It needs big money spent on it, Ross.'

'And ... Nicholas is going to spend this money?'

Her voice came out not so clear this time. 'Yes. His money and my property.'

'It's a lovely setting,' Ross said, 'but will people come all the way out there to eat when Salisbury is so near?'

'Nick thinks so, and – and I think he's right about that. He says if we advertise it in the right places, the appropriate magazines you know ... and of course many people know his restaurants anyway so he has the contacts.'

The waiter appeared at that moment with the menus. When he had gone Ross said softly, 'You said Nick thinks so. Don't you?'

'Oh Ross, I don't know, I honestly don't know. I trust his business sense implicitly, but I'm so worried about what it will do to the manor.'

She picked up the menu. 'We had better order, hadn't we?'

'Yes. What takes your fancy?'

She chose the duck pâté starter, the fresh salmon main course and a fruit cocktail dessert while Ross settled for chef's country soup, roast beef and apple pie.

'Wine or champagne?'

She raised her eyebrows. 'Glass of white wine please.'

'I'll stick with the glass,' he said, 'as I'm driving and you can have the rest of the bottle. I'll see you get safely home and into bed and no hanky-panky, I promise.'

He had the satisfaction of seeing her smile.

'What is worrying you about the conversion from dwelling place to restaurant, Maura?'

'I shouldn't really be talking like this because it's got to happen if I want to keep the place, and I do, Ross. I didn't quite realize until I came home how much I would hate to lose it. I've always loved it, but the shock of suddenly finding it was mine has made me more possessive than ever towards it, I think. It's not a mansion; in fact I suppose it's quite a small manor house as manor houses go; but it's just such a welcoming and warm home and I know I won't go on modelling for ever and...' She turned her head away and he said quietly, 'How much space would the restaurant take up?'

'That's the problem really. I imagined it being contained within the drawing room, which is pretty big, isn't it? I knew we would need to completely refurbish the kitchen to service the restaurant, and there is plenty of room to do that.'

'Yes?' he prompted when she stopped.

'I don't know. It's the rest of the house. Nick wants to take in the library and Uncle Tom's little study and he's even talking of using a couple of the bedrooms as meeting rooms.' She stopped suddenly. 'Look, forget I said all this, Ross. It's tremendously disloyal of me and nothing is really settled yet. It's just that looking at this place I realize that there are some really good conversions.'

'Mmm. But this has never been living accommodation. It's a bit different, Maura.'

Their first course arrived and he said gently, 'I'm glad it's not all signed and settled yet, so you still have options. Keep that thought in mind too. Now enjoy your meal, my love. It looks good. If I give you a spoonful of my soup, which smells delicious, can I have a slither of your pâté to taste?'

She laughed, 'You don't change, Ross, wherever you go in the world you would still be your natural self, wouldn't you?'

He put on a puzzled expression, 'I suppose so. Is that good or bad, Maura?'

'Oh it's *good*, Ross. Wonderfully good. Here,' she passed the little fork with a sizable piece of pâté on it over to him.

'Mm, mmm, delicious. Here, try some of this,' and he proffered his spoon and bowl.

'No thanks, I'm not really a soup person, Ross, for all that it smells tempting. Besides, I need to get into those slender dresses again next week.'

'You have a lovely figure. They don't make you diet in that modelling career of yours, do they?'

Giggling she said, 'No they don't make you do anything, but if I gorged myself on crisps and chocolate and roly-poly puddings and didn't fit the outfits I would simply be out of a job. Fortunately I can eat almost anything without gaining too many pounds, so I've never had a problem that way.'

When they left the restaurant they sat in the car for a long while talking about change of use for the manor.

'Obviously there is no other way or you wouldn't be contemplating it,' Ross said, 'and I respect that you have done some research into all this, but my gran always told me to look at the bleakest prospect because anything else would then be a bonus.'

'Wise lady, your gran. So what do you see as the bleakest prospect in this, Ross?'

'That it wouldn't attract enough customers, leaving you with nothing but debts at the end of it.'

'It's funny but I don't think there will be problems in getting people there, not given Nick's reputation and business acumen. It's the use of so much of the place that bothers me.'

'How many tables would you get in the drawing room, do you think?'

'Twenty, capable of seating six people each. We know that because Nick has measured it out. Could get more he says, but he doesn't want it crowded. It has to be in keeping with the manor house surroundings. "Elegant rather than seasidy" is how he described it the other evening.'

'He's right there, I'd say. Definitely not the place for kiss-me-quick hats.'

He glanced at her, snuggled in the seat beside him, but she didn't laugh or even smile as he had hoped. Instead she said in a serious tone, 'There will be tables for threes, fours and twos, of course, so there wouldn't be a hundred and twenty covers all the time. Sometimes only a third of that amount.'

'I understand that, but even so, if you can have most of them occupied all the time it would bring in a fair amount of people. Would you let them roam around the garden too?'

'Yes, we'd have meals in the rose garden too, during the summer.'

His arm stole around her shoulders and she didn't ask him not to, nor did she attempt to move away.

'Well, you can't do anything without planning permission these days, and it all takes an interminable time, so you have some space to think and talk about it.'

'That's what I'm worried about, Ross. The space it is going to use. If we lose the library and the study and some of the upstairs rooms too where will we live which is private?'

'Nicholas will live there with you?' His voice sounded odd, as though he were forcing the words out.

'I don't think so. He needs to be in town because of the other businesses. He's talking of putting a manager in, someone who lives locally. He dreams of having art exhibitions, modelling sessions and all kinds of culture things there...' Her voice broke and he pressed her shoulder and laid his cheek against her hair.

'It's *your* house, Maura my love, and no one can do anything to it without your consent.'

'But don't you see that if I withhold consent I shall lose the manor?'

She shifted her position so that she was gazing at his face.

'Oh Maura, my darling, if you look at me like that I shall kiss you and I'm trying so hard not to make you angry.'

He turned away and put his hands on the steering wheel. 'I'll take you home, then maybe we can talk some more.'

'I've already said too much. Looking at that lovely place this evening makes me wish the manor had a huge barn or stables that could be converted and the problems would all be solved.'

As they drove back to Picton they spoke about the countryside and the delicious meal they had enjoyed, and Maura tried not to imagine what might have happened if he *had* kissed her back there in the car park. The one emotion she knew she wasn't feeling tonight was anger.

There was no sign of Mrs Duffy when they got back, but two mugs, tea and coffee jars and a tin of biscuits were waiting on the working top near the kettle.

'She is a darling, isn't she, Ross?'

'She certainly is.' He was gazing around the kitchen as he spoke and mentally imagining it stripped of its homely warmth and kitted out in stainless steel and marble or formica working areas. This would be necessary, he thought, to run a fairly large restaurant here, but that didn't seem to be bothering Maura overmuch. It was the rest of the accommodation she was worried about. Well, if that man was bullying her he would have a certain Ross Edwards to deal with first.

Maura turned from the stove. 'Don't look so grim, Ross. I'm sorry I burdened you with all that, but don't worry about it. I shall deal with it and hope that I will be able to keep my inheritance. Actually it was a tremendous surprise to me because, although I never thought about it at length, somewhere at the back of my mind was the belief that when eventually Uncle Tom died my cousin Jim would be the new owner. He is Uncle Tom's stepson. If his mother was still alive she would have inherited the manor.'

'Jim hasn't been near the place for years,' said Ross. 'I can vouch for that because before I went to Australia I was often here and I would have known.'

Maura carried the mugs over to the wooden table in the centre of the room and Ross pulled a chair out for her. He pulled the next one over as close as he could to hers before sitting down. 'Your uncle didn't care much for Jim, but I expect you know that,' he said.

'I don't know a great deal about their relationship, Ross. I know Uncle Tom had been a widower for a number of years and that he married a woman who had a son, who was Jim. I only saw him a few times, I think, and that was when I was quite a small child. Mum was Uncle Tom's sister, there were only the two of them and Uncle Tom spoilt me then. I remember a really gorgeous doll he bought me one Christmas...' She bit her lip suddenly and his arm came round her.

'Well, you don't need to worry about Jim anyway, because he went off to Canada and I doubt if he'll ever be back. Darling can we...' as she turned to face him their lips met and Jim, Tom, Mrs Duffy, Nick and Jane all faded away. It was as though they were the only two people in the universe.

Chapter 14

The ringing of the telephone woke her just before seven next morning. There was an extension in the hall outside the bedroom. She threw back the sheet and hurried to answer it.

'Where the hell were you last night? No one there at all, not even that housekeeper you dote on.'

Holding the phone slightly away from her ear she said, 'I was out Nick and so was Mrs Duffy.'

'Till after half past eleven? With your housekeeper?'

'No,' she said sweetly, 'I wasn't with my housekeeper. She was back before me but she always takes her hearing aids out when she goes to bed, so she wouldn't have heard the phone.'

'I don't care what she does – where were you?'

'What is this, an inquisition? I grew up in this area remember, and I have friends here. People I haven't seen for some time. Is there anything else you want to know, Nicholas?'

There was a few seconds' silence before his voice, not quite so brash this time, was there again. 'Yes. How you're getting on with the business about the manor restaurant.'

'As well as can be expected, as they often say when you ring a hospital to enquire about a patient. You cannot hurry official-dom, as you should know. I went to each department and completed as much as it was possible to complete. Now, if you don't mind I'd like to get dressed. You woke me up.'

Ignoring her last remark he said, 'What are you doing today?'

'The same as yesterday with the depart-ments I didn't get to then. And before you enquire so pleasantly what time I will be back, I'm not exactly sure, but late afternoon I think. And I shall have an early night because I'm working at the crack of dawn tomorrow on an advert that needs to have the sunrise over the Thames as a background.'

'Sorry, Maura. I was worried, you see. Stuck down there without wheels and all that work to do on your own. I knew you'd manage, of course, but even so I was con-cerned for you. Did you take a taxi into Salisbury?'

'Naturally. Although there are buses from the village several times a day.'

When she replaced the receiver she was smiling. She never had been a person to be trodden down and Ross's remark last night, about the manor being *her* property came to the fore when Nick was being so bossy. In any case, she thought, from my point of view it doesn't matter if it takes ten weeks or ten months really. Dear old Nick, concerned for *me*? Concerned for what was happening about the manor, more likely. I have let myself be swept along by his urgency over this matter when at least half of it isn't necessary.

Later, just as she was going out there was a call from Ross. 'Busy all morning but I can get away to run you into Salisbury for your train any time after three,' he said. 'That be any use to you?'

'I can go by taxi, Ross.' But she said it without the anger she had used the other day. 'No need for you to turn out when you have work to do.'

'Nothing desperate, Maura. The farm isn't up and running properly yet, but plans are coming along well and I really would like to be able to take you to the station.'

This time her hesitation lasted less than a

minute. 'All right. About four o'clock, in case there's a lot of traffic hold-ups getting in.'

'I'll be over at three fifty five. That'll give us time to load your luggage.'

She giggled, 'One small soft-topped case and a handbag. See you later then, and thank you, Ross.'

She walked into the village without meeting anyone she knew, but while she was waiting for the Salisbury bus Eleanor Poole came by in her car. She stopped a little further along the road, backed the car to the bus stop and said peremptorily, 'Going to Salisbury Maura? Hop in, I'll give you a lift.'

It was easier to comply than to prevaricate and have the entire bus queue listening in, so giving an apologetic smile to the couple immediately behind her at the stop she slid into the seat next to Mrs Poole.

'So what has happened to your car?' the lady demanded.

'I'm not sure. Wasn't performing too well, so she's in for a small repair. Nothing too bad, I gather and it should be ready when I return.'

'And when is that?'

'Probably tomorrow, Mrs Poole. Depends on a couple of happenings in London as to whether I can stay down an extra few days.'

You'll never go to heaven my girl, she seemed to hear Mrs Duffy chiding her when she was caught out in a lie soon after she came to live with her uncle. She even remembered what it was about, and in a way the situation was similar to now. She had lied then to get out of answering a personal question about her parents' marriage when she was still in an extremely fragile state. She had found strength in her lie until Mrs Duffy had pulled her up about it. She was lying now to prevent awkward questions about the future of the manor house and hoped the implication about her London commitments would stop further questioning. It didn't.

'Well, we don't see much of you, my dear, but I suppose your career keeps you fairly busy. Are you planning to move down here eventually? Make the manor your main home and just keep a pad in London for work and odd visits back there?'

Maura wanted to giggle at the affected manner and strange choice of words Eleanor Poole had used. It sounded so false from that pseudo-posh voice. She said quietly, 'My modelling work takes me all over the country and abroad but a lot of it is in London itself. I need to be there for a while longer so as not to upset the schedule. So much of this is booked well ahead.'

'Of course. I understand that, but I heard that the manor was going to be sold. One of my friends mentioned only the other day, just before you arrived actually, that Mr Toning, the estate agent in the square, you know, had been seen coming out of your driveway. Not that it is anybody's business but yours my dear, but I do hope it is only a rumour,' she added quickly.

Nosy old bat, Maura thought, but she said, 'You should never listen to rumours Mrs Poole, they are usually grossly exaggerated. As a matter of fact I do know Mr Toning the estate agent and we often meet. He is a charming man.'

'Indeed he is, although I deplore these people using the Lord's Day for business. I understand so many estate agents sell more of their properties on a Sunday than on a normal working day. Signs of the times my dear, and traditionalists like me simply have to get used to it. Now tell me where you're going so I can drop you as near as possible.'

'I'm just on a shopping spree, so wherever you normally park will do fine thank you.'

Mrs Poole looked disappointed as she said, 'Very well. I'm going to my hairdresser,

I always have an early appointment to avoid the crush in town. I shall be approximately an hour, so if you would like a lift back...' she glanced at the clock on the dashboard.

Maura said quickly, 'That's very kind of you, Mrs Poole, but you know what it's like once you start browsing round the shops, so I shall probably not get back until well after lunch.'

'Well, enjoy your browsing, although with all the shops in London I'm surprised you want to wander around any more down here. Anyway should you decide you've had enough I will be here in just over an hour and only too happy to transport you back to the manor, my dear.'

As Maura hurried away from the car park and into the city she decided she would go into a shop first, just in case Eleanor Poole decided to watch her, because she was bound to be early for her hair appointment and it would be the sort of thing she might do. Once everything is settled with the manor and I really know how it is going to develop I will make a point of calling and telling her, she thought, because I don't want to make enemies, and she and her friends will probably frequent the restaurant anyway. It would be her kind of place.

'Naughty, naughty,' Maura murmured to herself. 'There's no real harm in her. She's a bit dated and self-important, that's all.'

Maura had a good morning. She talked to inspectors and brought back even more forms. 'Of course, someone will have to come and look at the wall you want to knock down. There are one or two instances here which will require attendance by an expert, but,' the middle-aged man studied the drawings in front of him, 'there seems to be no reason for it not going ahead and being granted. On paper that is. Let us look at dates.'

When she left Salisbury on the bus taking her back to Picton she felt happier than she had for some weeks. Things were moving ahead, yet she wasn't totally committed to the changes. She had not signed anything and she felt she had a breathing space. Change of use didn't sound as though it would cause a problem and in her view that could go ahead once they had the appropriate permissions. She would need it to if she was to keep the manor. If she could persuade Nick to do it this way and to talk about further projects when they saw how it was panning out she would feel happier about the changes which were going to be inevitable if she didn't sell.

She walked from the bus stop in the village and was back at the manor a little after three o'clock. She spent half an hour checking bills and business letters before trundling downstairs with her small case.

'Just time for a coffee before I leave, Mrs Duffy,' she said. 'Have one with me.'

'Thank you, miss. Oh but it is lovely to have you here. Do you know when you'll be back?'

'Not really. Because one of our models had a car accident I am taking her place so I have to be ready to change some of my plans when necessary. But within a couple of weeks, I hope. Don't let it stop you doing things and going places though. I'll ring and give you as much notice as possible when I'm coming and if you aren't here I'll ring you at your daughter's.'

'I'll be here, miss.'

Ross arrived just before ten minutes to four, exchanged a bit of banter with the housekeeper, then took Maura's luggage and put it in the boot of his car. They set off for Salisbury.

At the station he insisted on coming on to the platform with her. As they sat on the hard seat he edged as close as he could on the pretext of making room for others.

'You are incorrigible, Ross,' she said, laughing at him.

'Did you – erm, get on all right in Salisbury this morning, Maura?'

'Yes I did. I've got all the forms for change of use and it's simply a case now of deciding lay-out. I think we will get change of use without too much bother because it will be a quiet, classy business and as the manor stands a good distance from the main part of the village it really isn't going to affect anything there, is it?'

'That's right.' He was longing to ask if she also had forms for making two rooms into one large restaurant, but didn't want to spoil this new friendly footing they were on so he kept quiet and contented himself with saying, 'You'll let me know when you're coming down again, won't you?'

'If you like, but I shall probably have Nick with me next time.'

'Of course, if he is to be a partner in the business he'll need to sign things about that side of it. But I hope it won't stop me from paying you a visit.' He stood up abruptly as the London train was announced. By the carriage door he stood her case on the ground, put his arms round her and kissed her passionately.

Sitting by the window and watching the houses and gardens flash by she thought about Ross. He hadn't said he was back for good, but it seemed as if he was. He was talking of farming the land behind his grandmother's cottage, which was of course his now. Maura wasn't sure how much land there was; a fair bit, she thought. The cottage was really the last house in the village and beyond it were simply fields stretching as far as the eye could see. They must all belong to someone, unless they were common land. She shivered with pleasure as the memory of his kiss ran through her body yet again. This was foolish. If she and Nick were to run a restaurant in Picton and Ross was living in the village, either with or without Jane – she was still very hazy over what role Jane played in his life – then it was more than foolish, it was downright dangerous.

She played with the idea that Nick would go along with simply using the drawing room as a restaurant, plus the rose garden in summer, but there was a niggle that if he couldn't do it his way and make it larger and grander then he would pull out. If that happened she knew she would have to sell.

The only other way would be to find a job nearby which paid well enough for her to live at home.

It seemed as if she had been away for a long time instead of a couple of days. She felt totally relaxed and reasonably happy that there was a chance still of her being able to keep the manor house in one form or another without putting herself on the poverty line. The solicitor said there was enough money to maintain it as it was, with the gardener and the housekeeper, but there was very little left over for repairs and general maintenance. After the first euphoria of knowing it was hers she had soon acknowledged that it did need more money than she had coming in to bring it up to scratch and keep it in good order. As she joined the throng of people on the station and hurried towards the underground she let out a deep sigh for the peace and tranquillity she had left back at Picton.

Chapter 15

Ross walked slowly back to his car after waving Maura off on the train to London. He was elated at her change of attitude in just a few days. Smiling to himself as he hurried down the slope he recalled the high heels, the anger and embarrassment on her arrival. Then he thought about the warmth when he kissed her goodbye. No, not good-bye, au revoir. 'Please,' he said softly to a god he wasn't certain about.

He set about all his tasks at home with renewed energy because, for the first time since Maura had returned to the area, they seemed to be gelling together as they used to.

When she had left the village five years ago he believed she would be back within weeks, certainly three months at the utmost. When she wasn't he wrote to her, intending to get her address from her uncle and send the letter, but he kept putting it off and eventually he tore it up. He thought that if she didn't reply he would be cut off and if she did but was still angry with him, it would only make reconciliation more difficult. Now he wondered whether that reasoning was sound, but he'd known he couldn't offer her the kind of life she was dreaming about then. Not riches, but not poverty either. In a year or two she would have been twenty and maybe wanting to settle more, and he should have been expecting to be in a better position with his career by then. He also had not dreamed that she would never come home for a visit in all that time. He knew the quarrel with her uncle had been resolved, and to his mind it would be simple for him to pop in when she was visiting and resume the old camaraderie. It was what he had always done at the manor. Now that she had at last come back to Picton after Tom's death ... well, he admitted to himself, *I had reckoned without her stubbornness.*

He whistled as he went about his tasks that afternoon, and when Jane rang to say she would be back in Picton within a couple of days his cheerfulness must have communicated itself to her through his voice because she said, 'You sound very happy, Ross. Everything working well with Maura, or is it none of my business? Just say the word and I'll shut up.'

'I am happy, Jane. Maura has just returned to London but she and I are on friendly terms again. I'll tell you about it when I see you. The land business is plodding on too. Very slowly, but that's the way of councils and governments and all legal things over here. Let me know what train you'll be on when you leave and I'll meet it.'

'Great. Thanks. But if you have somewhere to go or something important to do I can always get a taxi or the bus or hitch a lift or something.'

His laugh rang out, a picture forming in his mind of when he had taken her into the station last week and Maura was just arriving. 'I know you can, but why waste the money when I can easily do the job.'

When he had returned from Australia, bringing the widow of one of his friends with him, he had really not been sure whether he would stay in England. He had loved Australia, both the vastness of the country and the bluntness of her people. He had learnt a great deal about different kinds of farming and had also taken several weeks' holiday before coming home. During these weeks he had visited the cities and beaches and met many people other than fellow farmers. Not that he could call himself an

Australian farmer because he hadn't owned a spadeful of land out there, but he had worked hard for a gritty but fair boss who told him before he left, 'There's a job here for you any time if you come back. I've no sons or daughters and in a few years I'll want to take it easier, get my drift?'

Ross said he did and was grateful. 'I need to go back to the old country and sort out a few things with a girl over there, but I'll keep in touch.'

The old farmer said quietly, 'She'll be a fool if she says no, but that's your business. Some English Sheilas do well out here but it's tougher on them than on the men and many can't take it. They get homesick. It can be a pretty lonely life.'

There was another side to all this, Ross thought. Whatever happened with Maura, he missed England himself. The good and the bad bits. Until he left he hadn't realized the extent of his love for his homeland, and although he knew he could settle and be content enough in Oz he also knew the hankering deep inside him would always be there. He would need to come home one day, even if it was years in the future.

Maura felt happy that evening too. She

176

looked through her post, took a call from her agent regarding next week's work and had just popped some thick sliced bread in the toaster when the bell rang. She was in two minds whether to ignore it but decided to check and went along the hall. She unhooked the chain on the front door and saw the shadow of a man through the frosted glass of the tiny porch. She called out, 'Who is it?'

'Ah, Maura. It's Jim.'

It seemed churlish not to let him in so she opened the porch door and said rather sharply, 'Jim, I'm sorry but I can only spare five minutes. I've just returned home and I have an appointment in less than half an hour.' Another lie, she thought. I seem to be making a habit of telling porkies lately.

He kissed her on both cheeks. 'That's a shame from my point of view, because I wanted a chance to talk to you without your boyfriend in attendance, as it were. Oh, nothing dodgy, cuz, but it's a bit inhibiting if he's here monitoring you, so to speak. And there's a couple of family things I want to discuss with you. Things you may not know because you were only a child when–'

'Jim, I really don't have time now, as I told you. Tell me the date you're going back to

Canada and give me your address or phone number and we'll have an evening together before you go, that's a promise.'

His face darkened but he recovered quickly and said, 'That's nice of you, Maura, because I do realize how busy you are with being the star attraction at Escudo now. I'm free most days because this is a sort of holiday for me, so anything I plan to do can be changed to a different day.'

Before she could answer the phone rang and, as she knew it would be, it was Nick.

'I've been back less than half an hour,' she told him, 'and my cousin Jim is here. He's just going, then I've an appointment as you know, but I'll phone you when I return if it's not too late.'

'What appointment's that, Maura?' Nick's voice was sharp and authoritative.

'Evening shoes and bags,' she improvised, 'I'd almost forgotten it but I have to do it, I'm committed.' She hoped that by saying that he would pick up the hint that she was simply trying to get rid of Jim quickly, and he did. His tone changed. 'OK, sweetie, I'll talk to you later.' In a slightly louder voice he added, 'Don't let that cousin of yours hold you up, tell him that some of us have to work. See you later, darling.'

Apart from her mobile she only had the one telephone, which was in the sitting room, and she hoped Jim had heard Nick's closing words. He had made no effort to move from the chair and, smiling brightly at him, she said, 'Well Jim, I'm sorry about this evening but you see how it is. Ring me before you go home and we'll have that get-together as I said, but this evening is a no-go, I'm afraid.'

Very reluctantly he stood up. 'What I want to talk to you about is important, Maura, so I hope you aren't trying to fob me off. Why can't we arrange a date now?'

'Because I've been away for several days and jobs and various other things have piled up. I have to clear the urgent ones, and you are here for another week or so, aren't you? So there's plenty of time for family talk.'

He lumbered out into the tiny hall, then turned to her suddenly and said, 'Where have you been, then, for these few days? Down to the manor?'

She almost said yes, then thought better of it. No point in fanning a situation and it was becoming increasingly clear to her that her cousin was angling for an invitation to Picton.

'I've been on a job. It involved a fair bit of

179

travelling and I'm really tired.'

'Yet you're still going out on another job?'

'It's my work, Jim. Models don't work office hours, you know.'

She had the front door open now and with a scowl on his face he went through. As soon as his shadow disappeared from her view through the smoky patterned glass she put the chain in position. Wearily she returned, put two fresh slices of bread in the toaster because the originals had popped up and gone cold. She reboiled the kettle, then went through and extinguished the light in the sitting room. She would eat her repast in the kitchen because she wouldn't put it past Jim to hang around and when she didn't appear outside and the light was still on in the front, put two and two together and come back. She didn't know him well but she definitely did not like him.

Chapter 16

'What the hell was that all about?' were Nick's opening words when she rang him back after rushing through her tea and toast.

'Uncle Tom's stepson from Canada turned up just as I got indoors and put the kettle on. I didn't want him here so I told him I had an appointment within half an hour to get rid of him. You played along nicely Nick, thanks.'

'I realized that's what you were doing, of course, but what on earth made you let him in anyway?'

'I couldn't leave him on the doorstep. It would have seemed so bad mannered I suppose. After all, he is family.'

'Listen Maura, you've not had much to do with him for years, have you?' Without waiting for an answer he went on, 'So why has he suddenly come out of the woodwork now? I'll tell you why. Because now that you are a woman of property he wants to be in on the act. I can spot his sort a mile off. He's after a share of the manor – no doubt of it. Don't let him into your flat again and whatever you do don't let him near the manor house. He'll take everything of value down there if he gets half a chance and–'

'Nick, please stop there. I'm not stupid, you know. Inviting him in here for ten minutes is nothing like asking him for a weekend in Picton. He *is* Uncle Tom's stepson–'

'Precisely. I expect he thinks he should have had your legacy–'

'I'm too tired to argue tonight, Nick. Let it go. I'll catch up with you tomorrow.'

'You haven't told me how you got on with all the arrangements in Salisbury yet.'

'It went quite well. I'll be in to see you tomorrow lunchtime. Where will you be?'

'That's no answer. How long is it going to take to fill me in on what's happening now? I have a vested interest, remember it's my money that's involved.'

'For heaven's sake, Nick, don't be so bombastic with me. We're both involved and it went all right. Now I'm going to get some sleep and I'll call in to Nick's Palace tomorrow lunchtime. If you aren't going to be there leave a message to say where you are and we can catch up later. Goodnight.' She replaced the receiver softly on to its cradle, curbing her instinct to bang it down. She stood looking at it for a few moments, half-expecting it to ring with an angry Nicholas Page at the other end of the line, but it didn't.

Maura slept fitfully, not wanting to believe Nick's interpretation of Jim's sudden appearance in England, yet already more than half-believing it herself. She had thought his interest and visit to Britain at this time was not coincidence. There were a lot of things that didn't quite tie up. Mostly that he said he had seen his stepfather on his previous visit, yet Uncle Tom had not mentioned a word to her. Surely he would have done so. He used to tell her all the gossip and happenings in the village. Who had been married, who had died, and the latest cricket scores for the Picton Pitchers, of which he was president. He would surely have mentioned that his stepson had been over from Canada.

She tried to remember anything he had ever said about Jim but she couldn't. The row, whatever it was about, was finished and done with by the time she came to live at the manor. She recalled her parents making reference to it years before they died and she went to live with Uncle Tom, but she couldn't recall what was said, only that there had been a huge 'bust-up'. She could actually picture her mother now when she said it, because new words fascinated her and she asked them what a bust-up was. Her father had laughed. A lovely, deep, gruff sound that she hadn't thought about for years. 'It's just a quarrel, Maura. Come on now, time you were in bed.'

Strange how real that scene was in her mind tonight. But of course she wasn't told what the argument, the 'bust-up', an expression she used often with her dolls afterwards, was about. She tossed around in her bed and eventually went to sleep to dream about that first home she'd known and her bedroom decorated in pale blue and the shelves with her books and jigsaw puzzles on.

It was just after two when she left the Escudo building the following day and went along to Nick's Palace.

'Let's go upstairs and talk,' he said briskly, kissing her rather casually.

The rooms in his flat above the restaurant were three times the size of Maura's. There was a sitting room, a master bedroom with en suite, two fairly roomy single bedrooms, one of which he used as an office, a bathroom and toilet and a kitchen. The flat was sumptuously furnished and there was a balcony outside the sitting room wide enough for two white ironwork tables (one each end) and four chairs, plus a few pot plants. It looked down into the street and often they would sit there in the late evening and watch people arriving at Nick's Palace for a meal.

Today they sat in the cream-leather armchairs in the sitting room. 'Have you eaten, Maura?' he asked as soon as she arrived.

'Yes thanks, I had a sandwich before I left work, but a cup of tea would go down well.'

He went into the kitchen and returned shortly afterwards with two mugs of tea on a tray with an assortment of biscuits.

'Just the cuppa, thanks.'

'Well, how much further forward are we?'

'Change of use is pretty certain. They want to know if we would be prepared to use part or all of the front lawn as a car park because they don't want a bottleneck in the lane.'

He looked up sharply, 'And what did you say to that?'

It was a delicious moment for her and she waited and watched him for some while before she answered. 'I said I had no objections as long as there wasn't a complete ban on parking in the lane. No yellow lines suddenly appearing or anything like that. I was quite firm about it because the lane doesn't carry much traffic. There is only us and a couple of cottages further along, and people have always been able to park there.'

For the first time Nick showed some enthusiasm. 'Good work, Maura. What else? How about the drawing room and the library?'

Drawing in a deep breath she said, 'I haven't actually filled in or signed anything about that yet because, as you know, I'm not entirely happy about it.'

'But we went through all that and it is going to be the making of the place.' His Adam's apple was moving rapidly as she said, '*You* went through it, Nick. You know I was unhappy with doing that and I think we should start with the drawing room as the restaurant and the rose garden as an extra in the summer and see how it goes. We can talk more about knocking down walls and expanding once we see how it works and if we get the customers.'

'And have all the disruption, which would probably mean closing for at least a week, probably more, and losing business when it could be done before we open. It's a short-sighted view. It needs to start as it means to go on, a fabulous classy place with lots of room and–'

'I'm not having the library wall knocked down until we see if it is necessary.'

'I shall have to go down and see them myself – it's such a simple thing, Maura; you're letting sentiment get in the way of common sense again. I'm surprised at you.'

'You know how I feel about it, Nick. Let's not run before we can walk. It will be less costly too.'

'That is not a valid argument, Maura. How do you suppose I've built up my business? By being bold and using all the resources available. I've thought about the upstairs, too, while you've been gone and have come to the conclusion that it can wait until we're rolling before offering conference facilities and room hire. That won't cost a lot anyway, nothing structural, just buying suitable chairs and tables. Possibly we'd need to put in another toilet, there's only one up there, isn't there, but it shouldn't be too expensive and–'

Maura, who had only stayed silent because her voice seemed to have physically deserted

187

her while he was speaking, suddenly found it again.

'Nick, I have to be by the Serpentine at four o'clock for a photo shoot. Everything is moving forward in Wiltshire with regard to planning permissions and we need to wait now for them to come through. There is no point in keeping on going over things like this.'

As she moved towards the door he blocked the way and put his arms around her. 'We'll go down together one day next week and get this project moving. We can look at all the alternatives while we're there, too. Although I still maintain that our best option is drawing room and library into one I'm willing to have a rethink, of course I am.' He kissed her deeply before releasing her from his hold. 'I'll come over to your flat later this evening and see which day we are both free for a trip to Salisbury and Picton. We could always go late afternoon when you've finished work, spend the night at the manor and be on the council offices doorstep as soon as they open the following morning. I'm sure we could come away with most of it sorted. We don't want to miss the next planning committee meeting. It is, after all, in both our interests, Maura.'

He locked the flat and walked downstairs with her. As they reached the bottom he glanced into the crowded restaurant, 'It's a good sight, isn't it, darling,' he said. 'I know how much you want to keep the manor house and you can do it with just a little compromise, my sweet.'

Chapter 17

Maura wished she knew exactly what part Jane played in Ross's life. My own fault, she thought, I stop him talking about her and telling me things. It's all very well for him to say she is the widow of a friend and he is watching out for her while she's in England, but she is actually staying at the cottage with him, dammit. She could have stayed in Salisbury, or even Picton. She tried to remember whether the pub had rooms to let, but she couldn't. Probably not, it was quite small, but even so there was loads of accommodation in Salisbury. What was she supposed to think?

She strode along, feeling frustration in every step. There had been a time, a very short time, when she had seriously thought of committing herself to Nick and hoping it would work, but her dreams of Ross always intervened, even when she thought he was in Australia and possibly married. She knew now that even if Ross married someone else, she could never marry Nicholas Page or, indeed, anybody. It would be courting disaster. Her love for Ross Edwards stood in the way.

In her rational and very down-to-earth moments before she and Ross met again, she had wondered whether her seventeen-year-old self had mistaken a tremendously strong crush for the real thing, whether the excitement he generated throughout her whole being was because she was young and it was the first time she had experienced such a powerful emotion. Now she knew it wasn't any of that. Since they had met again and with their individual experiences over the past five years inside them, the chemistry, both physical and mental, was as rampant as it ever had been.

She felt sure that Ross had had at least as many other encounters as she'd had during the past five years, very possibly more, yet...

'Oops, sorry,' she said to the man she careered into.

'Should look where you're going. Young people these days have no manners, no consideration.' He hurried on and with a start she realized she was almost at her destination.

For the first time in her career her heart wasn't in the job. Her professional self turned this way and that, smiled and half-smiled, posed exactly as they requested, and ignored as usual the passers-by who stood around, nudging each other and gazing at the models as they were being photographed. There were three of them that afternoon and when the dresses they were wearing had been done the girls went to the van which was parked nearby and were each given a coat, flimsy scarf, lacy gloves and picture-hat for the next shoot. The final set involved the same dress but different shoes, no hats, coats or gloves and a letting down of long hair that had been fashioned into various styles. The results were good, showing a trio of outdoor-type girl-next-door-images.

When they were finished Maura telephoned Nicholas Page. 'Don't go to my flat this evening because I won't be there,' she said. 'I thought I'd pop in to see Esmeralda, the girl from Escudo's who was injured. I'll come into the Palace afterwards for a while.'

She went to the hospital to visit Esmeralda, who was surprisingly, still incarcerated. She seemed quite cheery and was undoubtedly pleased to see her.

'You are the only one from Escudo who has been in,' she said. 'A couple of the others have phoned and left a get-well-quick-we-miss-you message. I suppose I sound cynical, but they don't really care. Well, most of them don't. It's a cut-throat business, isn't it, Maura, and I'm not sure I even want to go back to modelling when I eventually leave here. That is if I am fit enough. I'm pretty disillusioned with it all.'

Ignoring the last part of her remark Maura said, 'How soon do the doctors think you *will* be fit enough to return to the catwalk?' As soon as the words were out of her mouth she realized how they sounded, but it was too late to retract them.

'They were talking about six months. Oh I shall be leaving here long before that. I am apparently doing very well medically, but I mustn't stand for long and I will need to be careful for at least three months before I tackle anything like that again. But the senior doctor here, I call him "the chief", said that in six months' time I should be able to return to work.' She suddenly grinned at Maura, looking quite unlike the sophisticated and aloof mannequin from the salon. 'So your job is safe for quite a while. And Craig hasn't been in to see me once. He sent an enormous bouquet of flowers. Embarrassingly large – the nurses split them up and used every vase in the place. Oh yes, he telephoned too. Just once to check I hadn't died, I think.' A sad expression spread over her face and her eyes, usually so bright, definitely dimmed for a few seconds as she went on, 'Actually I'm not certain I shall go back even if I have the chance. That's between you and me, of course, but I've always fancied being an actress. I've been studying a couple of plays while I've been in here and I would love to have a go. Even dodgier than modelling, I expect, but I've had a little windfall since the accident and I can afford to coast for about a year, so I'm really tempted to try.'

Maura looked at the girl but refrained from encouraging or discouraging remarks. She reasoned that if she sounded keen about a change of career it would look as though she was afraid of losing her new status as top model at Escudo's. If she went the opposite way and urged Esmeralda not to risk the stage and films but to go back to her modelling it would sound as though she thought she couldn't act. So she said, 'I – erm – have inherited something too, Esmeralda. My uncle died and he left me his home near Salisbury.'

'But that won't affect your modelling, will it?'

'Sort of, because it's quite a property. Oh, not palatial, you understand, but largish. It's called the Manor House and is just a few miles outside Salisbury in Wiltshire.'

'Wow.' The girl sitting in a wheelchair by the side of the hospital bed said, 'Will you be lady of the manor, then?'

Maura laughed. 'Couldn't afford it. In fact I'm not sure I can afford to keep it because it's far too large for me alone; it's a family house really, and it needs a lot of repairs. I don't think there is anything major to be done, like the roof, you know, but practically everything else needs attention.'

'Was it your home before you came to London?'

'Yes. From the age of thirteen, anyway, when my parents died. My uncle took over my education, gave me a home, and...' To her dismay she felt tears trickling down her cheeks. 'I'm so sorry, Esmeralda,' she said, trying to blink them away and fishing in her bag for a handkerchief, 'but I love that

194

house, you see.'

'Oh, Maura, there must be something you can do to raise money so you can keep it. Could you rent it out while you're living in London? If you did it on a yearly basis it wouldn't tie it up for too long, would it?'

Maura gently touched her arm. She hadn't meant to blurt her troubles out like that, but she had seen a different side of Esmeralda since her visits to the hospital.

'We, that is Nicholas and I, do have a few ideas about running a business there and it would fit in with that and I could keep on the modelling career for a few years longer with any luck. We're talking about it at the moment, but you don't want to hear all my problems. You've got your own.'

'I'm fascinated, Maura. It's like a fairy tale, something out of a film or play. A real manor house. The squire and his lady. Do keep me updated, won't you? I love it.'

On the way back to Nick's Palace Maura thought about the posh and stiff star of the salon, Esmeralda. She wasn't standoffish at all. You can't really know people from the face they put on in public, she told herself.

When she reached Nick's Palace it was to find him in the restaurant deep in conversation with someone, so she waved her hand to him and went upstairs to the flat.

As she made herself a coffee she thought about actually owning a substantial property. Until her chat with Esmeralda this afternoon she hadn't really taken in that the manor house was completely hers. She knew it was, of course, the solicitor had told her, she had seen the will and the documents concerning the place, but the other side of her brain, the non-practical part, had not until this moment accepted that fact.

'Wow,' Esmeralda had said, and Maura suddenly saw her legacy in a completely different light. How Uncle Tom would laugh if she tried to explain that to him, and once more unexpected tears filled her eyes. Angrily she brushed them away and concentrated on the task of making some coffee. She had just carried it into the sitting room when Nick came bounding in.

'Sorry about that. Is there still some in the pot,' he said.

'Yes, I made a fresh brew.'

He walked over to where she was sitting, perched on the arm of the easy chair and kissed her.

'Want to eat in the restaurant or up here? I can get something sent up and we can catch up properly with each other.'

'Don't make them go to all that trouble. Let's eat downstairs, Nick. I'm not all that hungry anyway.'

He looked disappointed but seemed determined to please her. 'OK darling. And you can tell me properly the latest on the situation for the Manor House Restaurant. If it gets too noisy we can continue up here afterwards.'

'I told you all that earlier this afternoon,' she said, smiling at him. 'You really are the most persistent person I know, Nicholas Page, and you have so little patience.' A spasm of annoyance crossed his face but he turned the pursed lips into a sort of smile, leant over and lightly kissed her again.

They had a table for two tucked away in a corner. 'What days are you free next week, my love? I can tie in with most I think, and it will be a little holiday for us as well as being able to sort out the details of how we can manage the new project to the best advantage for us both.'

'It is all under way now, Nick. We simply have to play a waiting game. If you want to knock the library and drawing room into one and generally restructure the manor, then I'm sorry, but the deal's off.'

'Look Maura, on its own the drawing

room will make a pretty good restaurant, but with the library thrown in it will make a fabulous one. Trust me, darling. Just look around you at this place and you'll see how well it works.'

The waiter brought their meals and when he had gone Nick said, 'I have compromised. I told you earlier that we would leave plans for upstairs until we had the place up and running and then talk more about it, but you don't seem to be co-operating at all now, Maura.' He jabbed his fork into a succulent piece of meat. 'It will save me money to do it your way, but we'd be restricting our potential by having a much smaller place. However, it is your property at the moment and if we are to open in the autumn there isn't much else I can do.'

Chapter 18

Her cousin Jim was waiting for Maura a couple of days later when she left the Escudo building.

'Fancy a cup of tea?' he said. 'There's a nice little place I know a few turnings along from here.'

Maura really wanted to get home but felt a bit guilty at not doing something about offering hospitality. After all, he was her cousin, even though she had so little knowledge about him and knew there had been a split in the family in the past.

'All right, Jim, lead the way.' She thought it would be best to have a tête-à-tête with him in a café rather than have him in the flat where he might try to linger as he had on the only other occasion he had been there.

'That's great, cuz,' he said, suddenly grabbing her hand and hurrying her along Oxford Street. It was actually a ten minute fast walk down the side street and into two more narrow roads before they came to a row of four shops. One was a general store, one a tattooist, the next a bookie and last of all the café, which was on the corner of another road. There were some stone steps attached to the side of the café which led to a red door, and attached to the rather wonky-looking rail at the side was a notice which read, *Dressmaker*. Although it was in need of a coat of paint, the café did have a clean net curtain in the window and once inside Maura saw that the three Formica tables and plastic chairs the place contained were spotless. There was a counter along the back with a couple of machines gently hissing away, but no customers.

Jim pulled a chair out for her, then went over to the counter and banged his fists on it hard.

'All right, all right, I'm coming.' The woman who sauntered through the bead curtain was a peroxide blonde who looked to be in her forties.

'Oh, it's you, Jim,' she said. 'Might have known; making enough racket to wake the dead.'

Completely ignoring her remark he said, 'Doris, this is my cousin, Maura from Wiltshire. Tom's niece, you know.'

'Pleased ter meet you. You up for the day? Oh, you're the one that's the model, are you? You've certainly got the figure for it. Wish I was as slim as that.'

Jim turned to face Maura. 'Doris and her husband run this little place for an elderly widow. They are all old friends of mine.' Turning back to Doris he said, 'Two teas please, luv.'

Almost as an afterthought he said to Maura, 'Tea all right or would you rather have coffee or hot chocolate?'

'Tea will be fine, Jim.'

The woman set the machine going faster, then disappeared behind the curtain at the back. When she returned Jim walked over to the counter and a few moments later came back with two mugs of tea.

'I've known Doris and her family for years,' he said. 'Good hearted people they are. They don't live here, the woman upstairs, the dressmaker, is the owner but I always try to pop in a few times when I'm in England. Just hark at me. You don't want to listen to all this nonsense. Tell me about what you've been doing and how the manor is looking.'

'What I've been doing?' She smiled. 'Mostly work for me, Jim.'

'And Picton. Seems ages since I was there. How's the old place looking?'

'It's fine. The sort of environment that never changes really. Some new people in the village since I lived there but many of the old families are going strong. How long is it since you were over here?'

'I come every year, sometimes more than once, but I don't manage to get to Wiltshire on every visit. I'm usually over on business, and of course that has to take precedence over everything else.' He paused with the mug of tea halfway to his lips. 'Actually I've almost finished the negotiating I had to do this time. It went better and much faster than I expected, so I'll be able to stay on a few days extra and maybe come and see the old homestead. When are you going down next? I daresay I could fit it in to come with you then. Won't seem the same without old Tom of course, but there it is. I'm so glad I caught up with him last year.'

When she didn't reply he said, 'That old housekeeper of his still there?'

'Wasn't she there last year?'

'Yes, but I didn't see her. Think he'd given her the day off so we could spend time together. We had a good old chinwag, just the two of us.'

The shop door opened and a young man came in. He was casually dressed in jeans and black T-shirt. He walked past them slowly, went to the counter and a few moments later sat at the table furthest away from theirs. She saw him looking at her and it made her feel uncomfortable. Turning to Jim she said quietly, 'I'm not sure when I'm going down again so perhaps we'd better leave it until you're next in England.'

'Oh, come on, cuz. I only want to have a look at the place again. It could be two or three years before my next visit. Call it foolish sentiment if you like, but,' he leant closer to her and she saw the only other customer in the café staring at them, 'well, it would be nice to take a few pics and renew my memories of the place. It featured a lot in my life when I was younger and to tell you the truth I expected it to be mine when Tom died. After all, he was married to my mother and he always said it would be. I can see him now. "Jim, my boy," he used to say, "all this will be yours one day. The house, the land and the prestige!" I've not made a fuss or anything, but it's a bit galling to find he left it to you after all that.'

Maura quickly finished her drink and stood up. 'I think we had better be going, Jim. I have things to do this evening. Thanks for the tea.'

She noticed the other occupant of the café looking at her intently and quickly she turned her head away. Outside once more she touched Jim's hand lightly, 'I'm sorry to seem awkward but I truly do have so much model work at present. I've taken on extra, you see, and I can't get down there myself for a time.'

'How about telling the housekeeper that I'm having a day or two looking at old haunts. She can't have much to do if no one's actually living there now.'

'I don't think so, Jim.'

'Well I'm surprised at you, Maura. Tom used to say you were a lovely generous girl and you won't even invite me to my old home. Either he was wrong or the high life here has gone to your head.' They were almost back into Oxford Street, and he said suddenly, 'Are you marrying that chap I met at your place?'

She felt her anger rising. 'That is not your business, Jim.'

'Yes it is. Why should a stranger have what is rightfully mine?'

Maura stopped walking and Jim, who was almost a step ahead of her, had to turn quickly.

She drew in a deep breath and willed herself not to lose her temper. 'The manor house is *not* rightfully yours. Uncle Tom left it to me and I am not going to be intimidated by these veiled threats of yours.' She set off with long strides but he kept pace with her.

'Don't let's quarrel,' he said. 'I simply wanted to talk to you alone about the legacy. I mean, if that later will turned up you would be the one in my position now, wouldn't you?'

'I don't believe there is a later will. Nor

that you saw Uncle Tom last year – he would have told me.'

'Oh, that's nice, that is. I take the trouble to look you out, make sure you're OK because we do belong to the same family and you were a sweet kid, and what do I get for my trouble? You calling me a liar. Well you may be a top model, Maura, but you're bottom of the league when it comes to friendliness and hospitality. Afraid I shall claim the manor, are you? Well I had no intention of doing so. I have my own life and thriving business interests out there in Canada, but your attitude makes me think I might see a solicitor now–'

'Hold your horses, Jim. You can't claim something that wasn't yours in the first place. Uncle Tom was meticulous in his dealings with laws, have you forgotten he was a solicitor? Claim away if you want, but it will cost you a lot of money and the manor will still belong to me at the end of any dispute.' She strode off and was soon lost to his sight amongst the crowds in Oxford Street.

Jim turned back into the little streets and returned to the café. He went up the stairs at the side and banged on the red door.

'Now what is it?' Doris said as he barged in. 'And don't put that evil eye on me. I did what you asked and got Andy to study her. He'd know her anywhere now. Here.' She picked a rough sketch from the table in the centre of the room and thrust it at him. 'That boy missed his vocation, he did. Should have gone to art school. That's a spitting image, that is.' She snatched it back and studied it again. 'So have you got yourself an invite?'

'Would I be feeling like this if I had? Use your head, woman.'

'No good taking it out on me, Jim. So, what's the plan now, then?'

'Not sure yet. Don't want to use anything drastic to start with or things might get complicated. Kidnap could be simple. I know where she lives and where she works, but we'd have the responsibility of keeping her under wraps and not letting her know I had anything to do with it. None of that would be easy. Let it ride for a day or two. Meanwhile I'll keep my eye on these restaurants her boyfriend owns. She's not wearing a ring of any kind so I could chat her up, although we had a bit of a row today, so that mightn't work now.'

Jim picked up the sketch which Doris had laid on the table. He looked at it closely again.

'I've got an idea,' he said, excitement seeping into his voice. 'Get her boss to commission a portrait of her from Andy against the setting of the manor house and–'

'Can't see what good that would do.'

'Because you've no imagination and very little intellect. It would gain us entry to the manor, woman, and what a wonderful headquarters for our little game that would be.' He rubbed his hands together gleefully. 'Ah, Maura, my fine madam, you don't know what's about to hit you.'

Chapter 19

Back in his digs in Mile End Road Jim surveyed the shabby room. Why did all his schemes come to nothing? Well, this one wouldn't. This was going to be the one that broke the pattern, the one that at last got him the sort of lifestyle he had always dreamed about. He'd show those crooks back home in Canada that he knew what he was doing. He had to get it sorted on this trip. The bank raid was being planned for two months' time and every last detail needed to be in place. None of them knew he was Tom Wareham's stepson. He had reverted to his mother's name after the big row, and once he had paid them off they would never find him again. He had actually told them he was going to Scotland, where he had relatives. The three of them had already agreed that the money would be equally divided and then each would go their own way. There must be no visible connection between them. If he returned to Salisbury as Jim Wareham the few people there who remembered him as Tom's stepson would think he had now sown his wild oats and settled down. In due course he would sell the manor and travel. But for at least six months he would need to keep a quiet profile and not be seen to be splashing out. The manor was the perfect place to do this and to conceal all the banknotes too. As he would be the one to divide the loot he planned to make sure that it was on a one for you, one for you and two for me basis. By the time they'd counted their bundles of notes they would be back in Canada and he could be anywhere in the world. Pity there had to be three of them in it, but it was far too big for him to manage alone and they couldn't betray him without involving themselves. They wouldn't be able to find him either, because neither of them had an inkling about the Wiltshire connection nor did they know his other name or the fact that he had a recently deceased stepfather with money. He had been careful on that score. They knew his mother had been dead many years and that he was a bit of a loner. So far none of his schemes had worked, but with the help of the safe-blower and his racing-driver mate he was confident about this one. Anyway, it was only right and proper that he had the lion's share because he was the brains behind the raid and they were the labourers.

When the manor was his he would sack that old housekeeper and install Doris and her son Andy. Andy would be useful to keep the grounds in order and Doris could see to the domestic arrangements. Yes, it could work out very nicely. Neither of them knew about the money he would have from the Canadian bank robbery, and the manor house was a perfect place to store the 'old masters' that Andy painted from time to time. Why, you could even have them on show in a setting like that. It would be a good test to see if anyone did notice that they were not the genuine article. Then he would be able to make much of suing the art dealer he bought them from in London. Yes, that would be a daring thing to do. He rubbed his hands together like a child with a treat in store. When he sold the manor and moved away he would take on a new name, a complete new identity. He would travel the world, see all the places he had always wanted to visit, stay at the best hotels, have as many women as he fancied. Oh yes, the money would open so many doors. He probably need not be involved with the fraudulent paintings any more, although he actually enjoyed the thrill of the danger involved. At last life was showing signs of working in his favour, something it hadn't done for a long time.

There was a tiny niggle about Doris and Andy. He was ninety-nine per cent certain that they would never talk, after all, they were both more involved than he was with the fake masterpieces, they didn't know anything about the robberies and that was how he intended it to stay.

It was a shame they knew about the manor house, of course, but there was nothing he could do about that. To them he was simply fighting to keep an inheritance that should have been his. In Canada he was known as Anthony Woods. He had no bank account, he paid everything in cash and he steered clear of filling in any type of form. In anything from a few months to a few years someone might say, 'Whatever happened to that Tony Woods who used to hang around the bar with us?' They might speculate for five minutes before getting on with their lives. He had never got close to anyone wherever he lived.

Once he had acquired and then got shot of the manor he would be gone from Doris and Andy's lives too. 'Wonder where old Jim went,' one of them might say. 'He seems to have just disappeared. Odd.' Then they would shrug and forget about him. Andy would probably still spend his days in the National Gallery, studying and copying the old masters, and Doris would go along with whatever that old needlewoman in the flat above the shop told her to do. She always had a scheme on the go.

He did give a very fleeting thought to the possibility that he might not be able to gain possession of the manor house, but I'll have a damn good try, he thought. If that bit of my plan doesn't come off I shall need to store the notes because I can't use them for some time and there will be such a lot of them. I dare not risk putting them into a bank or a safe deposit. The manor house angle is by far the best scenario.

Pity Maura was so headstrong. Shame too that she seemed to be spoken for. He didn't want to make a play for her when someone else was in the offing because it would simply draw attention to him. If she hadn't had a man in tow, though, it would have been a great idea to chat her up. Safely married to her it wouldn't matter that the house was hers because he could come and go as he pleased. Do his travelling around the world on the pretext of his business commitments in Canada; they might even rub along well together and have some good times. It would be his open sesame to a higher level of living than he had experienced outside of those few months when he lived at the manor with his mother and Tom. Be a pretty safe environment for any shady deals he might still want to indulge in from time to time as well. There wouldn't be any financial necessity, of course, but something might come along that he couldn't resist.

Silently he cursed himself for messing up the last couple of hours. A thought bubbled into his head that if he apologized to her, on the pretext that his emotions had got the better of him because of his feelings for his 'dear old stepdad and the home he had loved', he might not cut off all communication in that direction. Talk of contesting the will had to remain just idle talk because he couldn't afford the fees to actually do it, although Maura wouldn't know that. Already the tone of the letter he could send her was forming in his mind. Not too 'humble pie' but apologetic enough to sound genuine without going over the top.

Maura was angry as she made her way to Nick's Palace. Angry with herself as much as with Jim. Allowing herself to be lured into that strange little café in a back street where there would obviously never be any passing trade. So what did that woman, Doris, do there? The only other customer, the chap who came in and spent all the time staring at her, obviously knew the place. *Drugs*, she thought, the sudden revelation making her stop so suddenly that someone behind bumped into her.

After the apologies she set off once more, determined not to think about this situation until she reached her destination. She looked into the restaurant and checked that Nick wasn't down there, before going upstairs to the flat. Nick was in his office; several sheets of paper were strewn over the desk, and each one was a sketch of a different room in the manor house in Picton.

'Hi,' he said, 'I'm trying to work out the best way to have the maximum space by using only the rooms you designate. There are many disadvantages and as I see it only one advantage.'

'What's the advantage, Nick?' The words were out before she realized and he grinned at her.

'That you will have all the space you want for your own accommodation. Though why you need all that when it could be earning money for the upkeep of the manor is beyond me.'

'Well, we don't have to go ahead with it. If we do it we want it to be a success and if you have those kinds of doubts then do what I said the other day and I'll sell the place anyway.'

He walked over, put an arm loosely about her shoulders and kissed her nose. 'Now don't be like that. Look,' he indicated the drawings on his desk, 'I am trying hard to compromise. If we begin with only using the drawing room as a restaurant, we could eventually turn the summerhouse into a sort of annexe to it. Not so good in the winter weather because it would be a possibly cold and wet walk through, but we could make a special feature of it. Have it as a themed annexe, the luxury wing of the Manor Restaurant, perhaps. Serve cold meals, seafood platters, beautifully decorated as they do in France, wonderfully exotic salads, and of course lots of mouth-watering desserts. No hot food, though, because of space and lack of proper cooking facilities.'

'I thought we'd agreed not to touch the summerhouse yet?'

'That was when we thought we'd have the library space too—'

'When *you* thought you'd have the library to use, Nick. I have never wanted that to be part of the restaurant.'

'Look, let's have a drink. I'm falling over backwards to accommodate your wishes, Maura, yet you try to thwart every move. You can only keep the manor if you make it pay. I can make it pay, I know I can. With your help, of course,' he added, his voice dropping to a quiet and reasonable tone. 'So why not bow to the inevitable and stop trying to block every move?'

Wearily she pushed her hand through her hair. 'Look, I've had one hell of a day. A busy outdoor session with half of London gaping at me, a run-in with cousin Jim and now this.'

'What sort of a run-in with your cousin, Maura?'

She walked into the kitchen and poured herself some coffee, bringing it back into the living room without asking if he wanted any.

'He's disputing my right to the manor,' she said as she sat down in one of the armchairs.

'That's ridiculous. It was left to you. What sort of claim has he got?'

She took a swallow of her coffee before answering him. 'He says there is a later will which names him as the heir.'

Chapter 20

'What time's your train, Jane?'

'Half past three. If the connections all work OK I should be with my friend around eight o'clock this evening. She and her husband are going to meet me the other end. It's good of you to take me to the station, Ross. I don't want to encroach on your time, though. I've got used to having to do things by myself, you know.'

'I know, but take the chance to be pampered a little while you can.' He gazed across the table and into her eyes which looked infinitely sad at that moment, and he knew she was thinking strongly about her husband.

'Tell you what, let's go a little earlier from here and get a nice lunch somewhere before your train is due. Allow ourselves plenty of time so we can eat at our own pace, eh?'

Jane grinned at him. 'And what would your girlfriend say to that?'

'She's not my girlfriend, more's the pity. I only wish she were.'

'That's as maybe, Ross, but she's in love with you just the same. Trust me, another woman knows the signs better than a man does.'

'Well, we won't go to her current beau's restaurant, anyway. The food there was spot on, though, the only time I went in. Beautifully presented and wonderfully cooked. I couldn't fault it, and if he does that in the manor house it will at least be in keeping with the place.'

'Is it all settled, Ross? Is Maura going to turn the manor house into a restaurant?'

'Mmm. I think so. If they can sort out their differences about which parts of the

217

place to use. Last time we spoke on the subject they were having a bit of a dispute about it. He wanted to use every available room, I believe, and Maura wanted to keep bits of it private.'

'Can't say I blame her. I've never seen inside, of course, but from what you've told me there is plenty of room for a classy eating-house and for her to live above the shop, as it were.'

'You know, in one way, Jane, it's a pity she was suddenly promoted to top model when that Esme – whatever she's called, was hurt in that car crash.'

'Esmeralda, the papers said. I can see your point, Ross. I suppose she could go on modelling and living in London and let Nicholas – is that his name? – run the place down here. So don't give up your hopes yet, my dear.'

'I doubt he'd do that. More likely to put a manager or manageress in.' Ross pushed back the chair and picked up his cup from the table. 'Thanks for listening, Jane. Now, chop chop, we need to get a move on if we're to get to town in time for a leisurely lunch before your train is due.'

Less than an hour later they were on their way to Salisbury station. Ross parked the car and trundled Jane's case along behind him as they made their way to the platform for the London train.

Maura always travelled by tube or bus when working anywhere in London because it was so much easier. She kept her little car for longer trips or for her modelling sessions outside the capital. Today she was working in Selfridges, where a short lunchtime display of Escudo evening wear was to be presented. She went to the powder room along with another model before the display was due to begin and as she came out she saw Ross and Jane going into the restaurant arm in arm. Her sharp intake of breath wasn't unnoticed by the other girl.

'What is it, Maura? You all right?'

Swallowing her emotional feelings as best she could Maura murmured, 'Yes, I'm fine. Just a sudden tickle in my throat.'

She couldn't resist glancing back just as Ross was pulling the chair out for Jane, who was laughing. It was obvious neither of them had seen her and for that she was grateful. She couldn't have borne a conversation with them and she had a show to do. Firmly she closed her mind to the little scene and prayed that they would not come along to watch the show.

Her prayers were answered, for there was no sign of them as the models strutted their stuff in the crowded store. When the performance was over and Maura was once more in her own clothes and heading out of Selfridges she allowed that vision of Jane with Ross to creep into her mind again.

What were they doing in London together, apart from having lunch? She didn't believe that they would have come simply for that. Were they here for the day or on a longer visit, and where were they staying? *It's none of your business,* she told herself sternly, *he is as much entitled to have a meal with Jane as I am to have one with Nick.*

She returned to the House of Escudo in sombre mood, and when Craig Escudo called her into the office she thought he was probably going to tell her that Esmeralda was returning to work, or that he had found another lead model. The one thing she didn't expect him to say was, 'Will you come to dinner with me tonight, Maura? There's a nice little place near Richmond which does quality cuisine?'

For a moment she was tempted to say yes, simply to spite Ross, but common sense prevailed. She smiled across the desk separating them from each other and said quietly, 'I'm sorry but I am going out with my fiancé this evening.'

He didn't look shattered, she thought later, and he only said, 'Maybe another time then? Contrary to what you may have heard I do like women. I'll see you here tomorrow. We have a bridal-gown show to organize.'

She felt his gaze on her back as she walked over to the door. As she opened it he said quietly, 'Don't worry about your job, Maura. I don't demote people who refuse me and you are a good model. I was watching you long before Esmeralda had her accident, you know.'

She half-turned and looked back at him. 'Thank you, Mr Escudo.'

'I think Craig sounds friendlier and you are, after all, my top model. Esmeralda calls me Craig, now you may do so too.'

'Thank you, Craig,' she said as she went through the door and closed it quietly behind her.

As she hurried along Oxford Street she wondered what the future held now. She knew that had she agreed to go to Richmond with him she would have well and truly been in Esmeralda's place, but that wasn't what she wanted. Top model – yes, but not the conditions that seemed to go with it.

She had no desire to be the pampered girl in the salon. In spite of his words Maura thought that Craig Escudo would drop her without a qualm if someone new came along who caught the mood of his creations – and the mood of the public too. Maybe this was her testing time. Perhaps he was ready to groom her for greater exposure and the thought of her picture on *Vogue* or *Tatler* or indeed on the cover of any of the expensive glossies was tempting. It would be the icing on the cake really, proof that she had made it to the top of her profession. But whom did she want that proof for?

In her mind was an image of Ross and Jane this afternoon, walking arm in arm into the restaurant, Ross attentively pulling the chair out for Jane, both of them oblivious, it seemed, to anything around them.

Was it for him that she wanted the proof? To show him she could do fine on her own? She remembered the flare-ups when he had tried to persuade her against striking out into a world he knew nothing about. It wasn't the glamorous environment she had imagined from reading about it, either, but she had worked and persevered and had

222

made good through her own efforts.

If she was dropped now she could possibly work for another fashion house or she could return to Picton, live at the manor and run the planned restaurant with Nick. She didn't have to marry him to do this; they could become business partners. His original idea of having a manager who lived in the area, together with a chef, would be the biggest expenses on the wage bill. Waiters, waitresses and cleaners and perhaps a gardening lad to help old Bill, would take care of the rest of the staff requirements.

She would need to watch her finances carefully. Certainly the business side of going back to the manor would need to pay. With Nicholas Page in overall charge she felt sure it would. He was a very hands-on entrepreneur.

Maura looked in to see how busy Nick was. She had told him she would do this on her way home, and when she walked into the vestibule and saw that all the tables were full and that Nick was not in evidence she decided to go home to her flat and ring him later. If she went upstairs it would mean a late journey back and she had several things she wanted to do this evening. The young lady at the till had seen her and smiled a greeting and, because Maura knew she had recently returned to work after having had a baby, she walked over to offer her congratulations. Two waiters came up within seconds to hand in payments and as Maura turned to go she caught a glimpse of a familiar back at a table half-hidden by one of the pillars in the corner. This was a table for two but from where she was standing the other chair would be tucked away inside the alcove and not visible to her. She could guess who the occupant was, though. She hurried outside and made her way home.

Feeling sick at heart Maura poured herself a gin and tonic before telephoning Nick.

'Hi sweetheart,' he said. 'Are you coming in tonight?'

'Too much to do here at home, Nick. I've had a busy day and tomorrow looks much the same.'

'It's pretty hectic here. Very busy all day downstairs but I'm not complaining.' They talked for almost three-quarters of an hour. Mostly about plans for the Manor Restaurant. He seemed to have accepted that they would not be using the library nor the upstairs at first, and even joked at one point during their chat that he would still have money in the bank by not doing so. 'I fancy that you will be voting for expansion once you see how popular this place is going to be,' he said. 'I have already told many influential people, several of whom have promised to come down for the opening, so we need to get things moving soon now, Maura.'

'I agree on that score, Nick. I'll get on the phone and see how plans are progressing. Probably go down for the day on Sunday and do some personal sorting out there.'

'We'll both go, Maura.'

She didn't protest. Now that she had come to terms with what was to happen at the manor she felt strangely calm. She thought Nick might again try to persuade her into marriage but they could work that out at the weekend. Without his financial assistance and his expertise in the catering business none of this could happen and she would need to sell her former home. With it she could pursue her modelling for as long as possible, or as long as she wanted or needed to anyway. On the other hand without her property Nick could not expand his empire into the countryside and she knew how much he now wanted to do this. His enthusiasm was catching but he never let it get in the way of his business sense.

It wasn't until she was in bed later that

night that she allowed those glimpses of Ross and Jane to creep into her inner vision. She had just begun to believe that Jane was really just a friend from Australia, as he said, but today had put paid to that idea completely. The Ross she remembered had always been so straightforward. He would never have said one thing and done the opposite. And he had said he loved her in more than words each time they met recently.

Everything seemed to be crowding in on her these last few months. Uncle Tom's death, meeting Ross again, promotion in her own career, Nick's desire to put their relationship on a permanent basis and Ross's nearness. That last most of all.

After seeing Jane off Ross went on the underground to the city for an appointment with a firm involved in getting the most and best out of a small farm. He had one more appointment while in London and that was with an old friend from his schooldays in Wiltshire. They had started school together; although David had left the area when he was about eight years old they had stayed in touch, not by frequently seeing each other, but keeping up with current jobs and addresses. They hadn't met since his return from Australia and Ross was looking forward to seeing his old chum again.

Their lives had taken very different paths. David was now a doctor in Harley Street and they had arranged to meet after his last appointment for the day and have a meal together. Ross planned to ring Maura, or even call on her depending what time it was when he was finished. The restaurant that David, who insisted on being host, chose for their meal was Nick's Palace.

When the two friends emerged after what both agreed was 'a meal worth paying for', they shook hands and went their separate ways. 'Now you are back in England you must come and have a meal with my wife and myself but she is abroad at present,' David said. 'That's why I didn't invite you to eat at our place today. I'm not the world's greatest cook and I usually dine out when Maria's away.'

Thinking about the possibility of the Manor Restaurant for entertaining guests Ross said, 'I'd like that, and perhaps you could get down to my area sometime in the next year too.'

Upon returning to his hotel he decided to telephone Maura, in case it wasn't conveni-ent to call on her. He had one more appointment in town before returning home tomorrow morning. Carefully he turned to the back page of the small notebook he carried in his top pocket. It was all there, her address and telephone number.

The number was engaged, so he waited five minutes before trying again. Forty minutes later, after his seventh attempt to speak to her Ross decided it wasn't meant to be this evening and gave up. It had seemed a shame to him to be in the same city and not try to see her but common sense prevailed and he was glad he hadn't gone on a fool's errand. She's probably talking to that twit who owns the place we ate in this evening, he thought.

He dreamt about Maura when he eventually fell asleep that night. In his dream she was seventeen again and he was dancing with her in the garden of the hotel during her birthday party. After a restless night he woke just after six in the morning with the taste of her last kiss just a few weeks ago on his lips. 'Maura, Maura, now I have something decent to offer you have I left it too late, my love, my only love,' he murmured.

Chapter 21

Jim wore the lovat-green trousers and blazer that he had sported when he waited for Maura outside Escudo's the evening he followed her home. They were smart and yet they were also casual enough for what he had in mind.

He had waited until his anger with Maura had collapsed a bit before deciding on this plan. He was after getting a job in one of her boyfriend's eating places. Preferably the posh West End one, but if necessary he would be willing to settle for one of the other two if it meant getting a foot in the door. In a settled job he would have some money, a commodity sadly lacking in his life at the moment. Of course, he didn't want to be a waiter for long; it would be a means to an end. He had spoken the truth when he said he used to work in large and expensive hotels in Canada.

He had simply omitted to say that he was the washer-up and had never progressed beyond this. However, he knew how to silver-serve and which side to serve from and practically everything else about being a waiter in a first-class establishment, because a man living on his wits needed to know as much as possible about as many things as possible. He was confident that he could do the job and that he could do it well and impress Mr Nicholas Page. If he played his cards skilfully it would only be a short time before he was offered a higher position. It would be easier if he had a managerial post, but if he didn't quickly progress from being one waiter among many it was still possible to do what he wanted.

These thoughts and plans were not because Jim wanted to work for his living. He only did that when there was absolutely no other option. In this instance it was because Nicholas Page had the keys to Maura's flat and Jim was a past master at getting hold of the items he most desired. It would be very much easier to steal them from inside the building and he would be earning money and probably getting free meals while doing it. He could easily have another key cut and return the original without anyone knowing about it if his luck held. It wouldn't take long and if the loss was discovered sooner than he hoped then he could help in the search for the missing key, but he didn't believe it would come to that. He was an expert at timing these things properly.

Jim didn't want to steal it from Maura because it would narrow the suspects, and there was safety in numbers by taking Nicholas Page's. The man wouldn't know it was gone and it would be back long before he next wanted to use it. The crucial point was learning where Page kept the key. The risk of detection was small if he was working alone. Jim preferred it when no other person was involved and a shiver of excitement shot through him as he chased the ideas around in his head.

Once he had the key it would be simple. Make sure Maura was working for several hours, then let himself into her flat and trash it. He wouldn't steal anything, unless there was some money lying around. Anything else could be traced more easily and there was too much at stake to risk it. No, he would empty drawers and pull off bedcovers. Put the plug into the sink in the kitchen and bathroom, and into the bath too and turn all the taps on. The only danger was being seen by neighbours or passers-by, and naturally he would make sure he wasn't. Another of his talents was the art of good disguise. That part would be a piece of cake, he thought.

The next step in his plan would be to offer to help in getting the place shipshape again. For this he would volunteer an acting friend 'who is currently resting'. This would be Andy, Doris's son from the café. They already knew about Maura and the manor house, so he wouldn't be telling them things he didn't want them to be aware of. Naturally Andy would do the job cheaply and well, and Maura would be so grateful for her cousin's help that she would invite him to the manor on her next trip there. A mention of having to find somewhere else to live for a couple of weeks while his rented place was being used by the owners ('I thought I would be back in Canada by the time they needed it and had only signed for the limited period.') should do the trick. To be on the safe side he would have his wallet 'stolen' when he was jostled in the tube station.

Once he was on the inside of the family so to speak, he would work out another plan to get rid of Maura and inherit the manor. A will signed by Thomas Wareham and witnessed by the doting housekeeper should do the trick, but this would take time. He was a competent forger and had in his possession several documents which bore his step-father's signature. Wait a minute though, the housekeeper could be the stumbling block here. He could get a sample signature easily enough once he was in the manor, but no matter how well he did her signature she would deny ever doing it. No, somebody else would have to have witnessed the will. A couple of the old man's colleagues from the club, or better still, two people who had known him but were now dead. There were bound to be bits and pieces with names and addresses on lying around the manor still. Maura wouldn't have had time yet to sort through everything and once he was in temporary residence there would be ample opportunities to poke about the place. What he had to concentrate on right now was the first step in this elaborate plan and that was the key to Maura's flat.

It's the only way, he thought, because the nice approach hasn't yielded anything at all. In fact, everyone to do with his cousin and the manor seemed to gang up against him. 'If you can't beat 'em, join 'em,' he muttered to himself as the spark of excitement he always felt in planning these dodgy moves came into play. That frisson of danger, of sailing close to the wind gave him an enormous boost.

He saw Nicholas Page the moment he walked in to the restaurant, but pretended he hadn't.

'Table for one, sir? Certainly. This way.' Jim followed the waiter through the restaurant to an alcove halfway down. This couldn't be better, he thought. From here he could see the full extent of the place. The table had a chair placed on each side of it and he chose the one facing away from the street at first. Having sussed out all the details he needed while looking that way he tried the other chair and faced upwards and into the street. While waiting for his meal he wondered where Nicholas kept the key. Probably in that upstairs flat, but he noticed there was a small office down here in the restaurant. It was at the back next to the toilets. It would be a doddle if he kept it there. As an employee he would have no difficulty in finding an excuse to go in. The flat upstairs would probably mean a break-in and that was best avoided. Someone might see him. He realized that the staff would be questioned and as the newest recruit he would be checked out more thoroughly than the others, but he felt very confident he could ride that. He had, after all, had years of practice.

He had declined a starter and chosen the main course only, for economic reasons, and he lingered over that. He went to the gents so he could look closely at the type of lock on the office door. He was a dab hand with locks, even if he did say so himself. Anyway, indoor ones were never as secure as outside ones. When he returned he signalled for his bill and walked slowly to the counter to pay. He saw Nicholas Page go to the girl at the second till, lean across and say something to her. She smiled at him, turned to a hook on the wall behind her and took down a sheaf of papers held together with a bulldog clip. Without looking round he went into the entrance hall and up the stairs to his flat.

It was tempting to try for an interview there and then, but Jim decided to go through the normal channels rather than disturb Nicholas now and risk a blunt refusal. Smiling broadly he left the restaurant, knowing now that Nicholas Page carried a key to his flat on his person. The key to Maura's flat could well be on the same ring. He decided against going round to the back of the building to check for a possible means of entry that way in case the restaurateur was looking out of the window at the back and saw him. He could do that reconnaissance sometime tomorrow after watching and checking that the proprietor was not in the vicinity; and if there was no other way he could turn up in disguise with an extending ladder and pretend to be checking all the windows in the properties along there. Simple enough then, with the right tool, to cut the glass from the frame and get himself in. The dodgy bit would be not having a look-out on the ground to make sure that Nicholas Page did not return and let himself in through the front entrance.

He knew all the likely places a man would put his keys and a quick search of the premises would reveal whether or not his cousin's boyfriend carried that particular one around with him too. Remembering the evening Nicholas had turned up suddenly at Maura's flat and rung the bell Jim recalled him saying, 'I came without my key.' As he walked home he chuckled quietly to himself.

Chapter 22

Maura and Nick drove down to Picton very late on Saturday night. 'If we can get as good a manager into the Manor Restaurant as I have up here in these three it will be great,' Nick said. 'I don't want to return to having to be in any place all the time. I thought we could concentrate on Picton until it's up and running, then put a manager in fairly quickly. I've a couple of people in mind who would be right for the job, but I'm not sure whether either of them would want to leave London on a long-term basis, so I rang and asked your Mrs Duffy to buy all the local papers for this week from around a fairly wide area. We can see what's what then and decide whom to approach when the time comes.'

Maura thought that rather high-handed of him, but she said nothing. The deed was done, after all, so not much point arguing about it now. She sat silently as Nick drove through the night. She felt a contentment she hadn't known for a while and knew it stemmed from the fact that now she should be able to keep the manor and her job, and not have too much alteration in the layout of the building. To retain the library and the upstairs was very important to her. The whole place was her little bit of heaven, but until she returned to see her legacy after Uncle Tom died she had not fully realized how much it meant to her. The fact that Ross was at present living in the village had ceased to be a difficulty. Even though she was sure her heartbeats doubled and sometimes tripled when he appeared she felt that she could cope with it. She would still be in London more than in Wiltshire for the foreseeable future, she thought. He professed to love her yet he still went around with Jane and it seemed to her that those two were far more than friends. She was the one who was holding back now. If there was no Jane in the offing she knew she would have succumbed to his advances, but there was no way that she was prepared to be a substitute when the other woman went off for a few days, as she had the other week. After all the silent years the attention he now gave her was unsettling but...

'You're so quiet I thought you were asleep.' Nick's voice startled her from her reverie and she looked across at him. His firm, strong hands were steady and relaxed on the steering wheel, his brown eyes concentrating on the road, and the smell of his aftershave faintly reaching her nostrils.

'I was thinking how good it was to be travelling at this time of night,' she said. 'It's as though we have the roads to ourselves.'

'Yes, it's great. You can really motor. We seem to be making headway with the restaurant project too. Frustrating until now but it's moving in the right direction and, given a bit of luck and no hold-ups with the alterations we could have the grand opening in the autumn after all.' His left hand reached out and patted her knee. 'Will be good to have a place in the country to come to when we want to get out of the city, won't it, darling?'

'I shall keep my flat on because of work, but yes, I'll spend as much of my spare time at the manor as I can. Esmeralda is well on the road to recovery so I'm not sure how much longer I will be in the top echelon at Escudo's. Although she says she wants to try her hand at acting I suspect she will need her modelling contacts too.'

She hadn't mentioned Craig Escudo's invitation and privately she thought that it was simply a matter of time before she was replaced, either when Esmeralda returned or he had found another face and figure he was happy with. It could even be before the next collection. Strangely enough, she thought, I don't mind. Five years ago I would have been devastated and now I'll probably welcome it and might even go for a job in Salisbury as Uncle Tom urged me to then. A flicker of sadness invaded her being because she could no longer tell him this.

She knew she could manage the Manor Restaurant and that Nick would be happy with this arrangement, but it would bind her to him more than she wanted. Since the scene with the engagement ring he had hinted once or twice about their lives together, but had not pursued the idea openly and she was glad. They worked well together and she saw no reason why they could not be business partners only. Her property and his restaurant. She had flirted with the idea of a more permanent relationship once but that was before she saw Ross again. She knew now that that was out of the question.

They went into the manor by the big oak front door. Maura had told Mrs Duffy to lock up and go to bed and that they would not need anything when they arrived. Nevertheless there was a large note on the hall table from the housekeeper to say there were cups set out in the kitchen and a freshly baked cake in the tin should they require it. The *Wiltshire Times* and the *Salisbury Journal* were on the table too. Maura read the note and smiled. 'Must remember to give her the money for these,' she said. Nick tucked the papers under his arm and picked up their overnight bags.

'Your housekeeper has a home apart from her quarters here, doesn't she?' he said.

'Not really, no. She has lived here for donkey's years.'

'I see.'

'Nick, Mrs Duffy comes with the property. If you have any ideas about turning her out, then forget them now. Don't even hint at it to her, because if you do then the deal is off and there will be no Manor House Restaurant. I mean it.'

'Oh for pity's sake don't be so uptight about it. It's something we can discuss when we get around to actually doing the alterations.'

'There is absolutely nothing to discuss, Nick. Mrs Duffy's room will remain just that, and while we're on that subject, she will be able to have meals in the restaurant

241

without paying. I will recompense the business for that.'

'I said we can discuss these kinds of arrangements when we get to them. The important thing now is to get the ball rolling, get the–'

'Nobody is going to roll any ball until we have the domestic situation sorted.'

'OK, OK. It's not a problem. I've already agreed to leave the upstairs for the present, so her room is safe. Let's concentrate on getting the main part of the restaurant ready. We can go into Salisbury tomorrow and not budge from any office until everything is finalized. It's to both our advantages sweetie. Agreed?'

'Of course. The sooner the better now, but I mean every word I've said and I'll not be moved from that.'

He sighed. 'Understood, Maura. Now let's get a few hours' sleep and be fresh for an early start tomorrow. I presume your wonder-woman will give us a hearty breakfast to start us off.'

She let the sarcasm go. For once she didn't feel the need to jump in again. Too much was at stake for him to do anything but what she wanted over this particular issue. Later, remembering Mrs Duffy's reaction and remarks after Nicholas's first visit, she thought that the housekeeper would probably take matters into her own hands and leave anyway, but that was a different matter altogether. She would never allow her to be pushed. The manor would be dear Duffy's home for as long as she wished it to be.

They went into Salisbury after breakfast on Saturday. In spite of his fighting talk of the previous evening Nick couldn't beard anyone in council offices because they weren't there. He did go to the builder they had earmarked for the transformation job. Because it was only the kitchen and a toilet block that they now needed it wouldn't take as long as they had at first supposed, and they already had the permissions for these. Someone from the council had been round to look and assess and had said 'yes' before leaving. Nick had had a letter confirming this and the builder promised to come along in the afternoon and give his estimate for doing the job. The proposed alterations had been published in the local newspapers and the plans were available to see in the council offices. Nobody had complained: 'Well, it won't interfere with any other building,' Nick had said to her, 'and often people don't bother to check these things. In any case it will be a great advantage to Picton and the whole area.'

Maura wasn't sure about this. With a car people could travel wherever they fancied but when, some days ago, she had mentioned this fact to Nicholas he had countered with, 'I know that, and people with cars will come from far and near to eat at the Manor Restaurant too. People from London, from Surrey, Sussex, Hampshire, Kent. You'll see, my love. It will be a focal point, like all the Harry's Bars around the globe are. In fact, once this has been going a couple of years we might even look for run-down old country properties which we can convert...'

She had smiled warmly at him then. 'That's what I've always liked about you, Nick, your enthusiasm and supreme confidence.'

'I'd hoped it was more than just that,' he had said. As he reached for her the telephone rang and to her relief he was caught up in his business life again.

Salisbury was busy on Saturday morning but they did all they wanted to. They bumped into Mrs Poole, who fortunately was hurrying to an appointment and couldn't stop to chat. Then they had lunch in a pub a short distance from the city. Maura remembered the one Ross had taken her to not so long ago, but she wanted to keep that one to herself.

Nicholas went round with the builder and Maura talked to Mrs Duffy about their plans. They were sitting in the drawing room with a cup of tea each and the older woman looked solemn. 'Forgive me asking, Miss Maura, but are you going to marry Mr Page?'

'No, but we will be business partners. The restaurant will be here in my property and he will finance and run it. Well, he'll probably put a manager in because he already has three catering businesses in London. It will be a first-class place, Mrs Duffy, a quality eating house,' she added as she saw the concerned look on the housekeeper's face.

'And will you live here?'

'Yes, when I'm home. I have my flat in London and of course I'm there most of the time when I'm working, but when I'm not then I shall be down here.'

'I see. Thank you for telling me.'

'It won't affect your accommodation, Mrs Duffy, nor mine. The restaurant will be in here and of course the kitchen will be refitted but everything upstairs will be exactly the same and that part of the house will be cordoned off and marked private.'

'Hmm. When is all this going to happen, miss?'

'In – in the autumn we hope. And of course you and I can have our meals down here at no cost and it won't be open all day; the times are something still to be worked out...' She ran out of words as she saw Mrs Duffy's expression.

'Well, I hope it works out for your sake, Miss Maura and–' She broke off and turned away suddenly.

'And what, Mrs D?' She used Ross's pet abbreviation unthinkingly.

'It isn't for me to say, of course, but I – well I was going to say that I'm glad you're not marrying him.'

Chapter 23

Ross saw the car coming from the lane that led to the manor house as he walked back from the village shop and post office. There were two people in it and although he was not close enough to see them clearly he knew that Maura was down and that she had Nicholas Page with her. It didn't pass him. It turned left out of the lane and zoomed off much too fast. As he came up to the lane he decided to call in and see how long they were to be here. Mrs D would tell him that – if she knew, of course. Quickening his pace and swinging the plastic bag of groceries in his hand he walked along the lane towards the manor.

Ten minutes later he was sitting by the scrubbed wooden table in the kitchen with a strong cup of tea and a fair-size slab of home-made fruitcake to eat. He hadn't intended to stop, just to find out how long Maura was to be in Picton, but when he tapped on the back door as usual he surprised an unusually sombre Mrs Duffy with his appearance.

'I've not come to hinder you, Mrs D,' he said. 'Simply to find out when Maura is returning to London.'

'Monday morning, I think. Come on in and have a cuppa.' She was on her way back indoors before he could protest that he wasn't stopping. He followed her into the kitchen.

'Sit you down. They've not been gone long.' She moved to the sink and stove. Her voice was heavy with tears as she turned from him to put the kettle on.

'Hey, what's up, Mrs D? You all right?'

She nodded, then brushed her eyes with the back of her hand. 'Yes.'

'Sure?'

She nodded. As she reached into the cupboard for the crockery she knocked a milk jug from the shelf. He leapt up and saved it before it fell to the floor. Her hand was trembling as she took it from him.

'Has that Nicholas Page upset you, Mrs Duffy? You can tell me, you know?'

'Not with words. It's – it's what they're intending to do.' There were tears in her eyes now and she blinked hard. 'It's none of my business, I know, but I can't stay and watch it happen Mr Ross – I just can't. I only knew for sure this morning.'

Ross felt a physical pain shoot through his body. 'Only knew what for sure, Mrs D?'

She looked down to the floor. 'This lovely old house is going to be a restaurant and my kitchen will be turned into a shiny steel workshop, and there'll be cloakrooms built all over the place for the customers to use and – and...'

'They're not turning you out, are they?' he said when she stopped to fight her tears. 'Here, sit down, I'll finish that.' He guided her to a chair.

248

'No, oh no, nothing like that. My room will be the same and I can eat in the restaurant every day without paying. As if I'd *want* to do that. I'd pay if I ate in any restaurant anyway. But I wouldn't stay here. I couldn't with that man in charge.' She put her head in her hands and wept. He patted her shoulder as they sat side by side and she sniffed and turned to him apologetically.

'I'm sorry. I'm all right now. Here, have some cake, I made it early this morning, it's cool now.' She rose and walked across to the worktop where a rich-looking fruitcake was on the cooling rack. Ross didn't think he would be able to swallow a crumb, he felt so choked up.

'When are they getting married?'

'They're not getting married. That's the only good thing about it. They're going to be business partners. He's going to run the restaurant and Miss Maura will keep her London flat and come down when she's not working. Oh, I shouldn't be talking like this to you but you're almost like one of the family, Mr Ross. And I feel so het up about it all.' She jumped up suddenly. 'You didn't put the cosy on the pot, the tea'll go cold.' She patted the multicoloured knitted tea cosy into place and when she turned back to face him she saw the big grin spreading over his face.

'They aren't getting married, did you say?'

'That's right. Miss Maura was quite clear on that. But he'll be in charge of the restaurant.'

Ross took a huge gulp of tea. 'Look, I've got to go. I've got a lot of work to do on the farm. May I take my piece of cake with me for later? I suddenly feel like eating again. And smile, Mrs D, because she's not marrying him and I've now got a home of my own I can offer her.'

'Oh, Mr Ross, maybe things aren't so bad after all, then.' Mrs Duffy jumped up, pulled off a sheet of kitchen roll and carefully wrapped his fruitcake. 'There you are, enjoy it.' As she handed it to him he put his arms round her and danced her to the door. 'And don't you worry about somewhere to live either. I've got plans for the farm and there's lots of space, it only needs organizing. As long as she doesn't marry that twit we'll both be all right. You take care now, Mrs D.' To her amazement he gently kissed her cheek before taking off, almost skipping like a young boy down the path.

'Your groceries,' she called, dashing back indoors for them. 'You can't live on cake alone.' For the first time that morning she laughed aloud.

Ross walked back to the farm and thought about his plans for it. Being able to buy that extra land adjoining his own had made all the difference. Of course there was a deal of work to do on it before it would produce anything for him but he had never been afraid of hard graft. The extra acreage would, he knew, make all the difference between being able to run a profitable small farm or a hobby style farm where anything he sold was a bonus but he would need to have another job as well.

Most of all he would be able to ask the girl he loved to marry him. The thought that she might say no never entered his head. If she wasn't going to marry Nicholas whatever his name was, then it was because she was still in love with him, and every indication he had had from her lately checked this out. In the solitude and quietness of his farm he let out a huge, 'YIPPEE.'

Salisbury was its usual busy Saturday self. The market was in full swing, parking was at a premium and when they had managed it and were leaving the car park Mrs Poole's voice assailed them.

'Why hello there, Maura and...' she turned towards Nick.

'Hello, Mrs Poole. This is Nicholas Page, a friend from London. Nick – Mrs Poole.' They chatted for a few moments, mostly about the weather and the contrast of a busy town from the peacefulness of Picton. Before they parted Mrs Poole trotted out her usual line whenever she saw Maura, almost as though it was a personal invitation from her.

'Shall we see you in church tomorrow my dear. I do hope so.'

As Maura was about to reply Nick said, 'Yes, of course, Mrs Poole. I am looking forward very much to meeting all Maura's hometown friends. We don't need to return to London until Monday morning.'

Maura was furious with him. Her anger reached bursting point on the way to the builder's office to arrange for him to call and check measurements and materials for the alterations.

'She's the biggest snob in Picton and not one of my particular friends as you so ingratiatingly intimated and now if we don't go to church tomorrow morning–'

'But we *are* going, aren't we, Maura? She may be a snob but she is exactly the one we need to spread the news of our restaurant. We will make a point of telling her the news first and very discreetly make sure she knows she is the first. She will alert all her county friends, and do lots of unpaid advertising for us. By the way has she a husband or is she a widow?'

In spite of her feelings Maura had to smile. 'You are incorrigible Nick. You use people for your own ends.'

'Of course I do. Most of us do, although it's often so wrapped up they would be surprised if you said so. I know I do and I'm not ashamed of it. You do too, or at least you did when you first came to London. There's nothing so very wrong with the idea after all. And if Mrs Poole brings in lots of business she will be treated with the deference she would want – I'm happy enough to do that. It will send up her stock with her friends and it will do us some good.'

'But it's so – so superficial Nick.'

'It's the way the world works, Maura, especially the business world. You didn't answer my question about her status.'

'To be honest, I'm not sure. I think she is a divorcee, something Uncle Tom said to me a long time ago seems to have stuck in my mind, but I believe she tells people she is a widow. It would only be the very old ones who may have known her husband who would really be aware. He was away a lot, abroad most of the time I think.'

'There you are then. We won't be telling any lies when we say we serve the best food for miles around, but we could do with a little help in getting people in there to begin with. Your Mrs Poole will do nicely. She will attract the people who can afford to dine at the manor, who will enjoy and appreciate both the menu and the ambiance of the place. We would be utterly stupid not to take advantage of her.'

The builder said he would come over after lunch, 'say three o'clock or thereabouts.'

'That will be fine,' Nick said, 'we are just going for a bite to eat ourselves now then we shall be returning to the manor. See you later.'

When Nick and Maura returned to the manor Mrs Duffy was out. Maura had said they wouldn't need anything except a bit of salad or some sandwiches for tea or supper. There was a note on the table, anchored by a vase of early roses. It read:

Dear Miss Maura, have gone to my daughter's

but will be back later this evening. There are sandwiches in the fridge and a fruitcake and some scones in the tin. Thank you, miss. E. Duffy.

Maura smiled and renewed her determination that Nick would not be allowed to push the housekeeper out of what had been her home and living for years.

The builder and the plumber arrived within five minutes of each other. They laid the plans on the kitchen table and proceeded to measure and pace the length and breadth of the area. Nick was taking part in the discussion but Maura wanted to stay to make sure nothing they hadn't already agreed was done. She sat quietly, watching and listening. It all seemed feasible. Of course it would look like the kitchens at Nick's other restaurants but that couldn't be helped. It would have a different purpose from the homely place where Mrs Duffy cooked. She accepted that, although she wasn't sure that the housekeeper would. Already Maura had been thinking along the lines of turning the small upstairs study into a kitchenette for her. It wouldn't be very roomy but large enough for one and she would have her privacy and could do and cook whatever she wanted, Maura thought.

Maura took her pocket diary from her handbag and they arranged a date for the builders to start work. It had to be fitted into her commitments, although Nick said he would be able to fill in down here some of the time if she was too busy.

'And of course Mrs Duffy can earn her keep by being here if neither of us can get away,' he said. Maura bit her lip and kept silent.

'We want a big opening in September,' Nick said as he escorted the builder out. 'Closer to the time we shall be advertising the date and I want your guarantee that everything will be on schedule.'

'You have it, Mr Page. If we hit any snags, which is unlikely, you will know about them in plenty of time for us all to have a rethink. But that won't happen. When Charley Simms gives his word it's like a solemn oath, I promise you. Your restaurant will be ready to open for business by the end of September of this year. No worries.'

Chapter 24

Jim wrote a letter to Nicholas Page applying for a job as a waiter in the Oxford Street restaurant. His money was getting dangerously low; he only had another couple of weeks in the rather grotty rooms he was renting and so far on this trip he had had to pay out for rather more than he bargained for. The original idea of contacting cousin Maura and charming her into letting him use the manor house as his base had failed miserably and he was growing more desperate each day. Which is why, when he had not had a reply after nine days, he went to the restaurant and asked to see Mr Nicholas Page.

As the girl at the desk was telling him that Mr Page was not available or even in the building but she would take a message, Nick strode in through the magnificent double glass doors of the reception area.

Jim rushed over and confronted him before he could disappear up the stairs to his flat.

'Nicholas,' he said, 'what luck seeing you. Did you receive my letter? It's Jim, Maura's cousin, you know. We met at her flat a few weeks ago.'

'Of course I know who you are, but we've no vacancies.'

As he moved away Jim followed and was about to say more when Nick, with one foot on the stairs now, said, *'No* vacancies. Not for chefs, waiters, nor even for sweepers-up. And I don't like being hustled this way on my own premises. Please leave now.' Then he was gone, disappearing round the bend in the stairs and Jim heard the unmistakable sound of his key in the door.

Turning, he saw the girl at the desk inside Nick's Palace looking at him and he swore quietly to himself. He glared at her, then stomped out into the street. Damn Nicholas Page and his high-profile eating-house. He didn't need them and he certainly wasn't going to be spoken to in that manner. Oh no, he'd show the upstart. He started to laugh as he pushed his way through the crowded street. I only wanted to work there to obtain the key to my own cousin's flat. How bizarre is that? he thought. It would have been a convoluted way of doing it and the appeal of it is rapidly wearing off. I'll get into the manor to stay somehow, though, and I'll get even with that pushy boyfriend too.

He stopped suddenly, causing people to bump into him. This produced various reactions, from anger to amazement, but this absolutely brilliant idea had struck him. If Maura were to finish with bloody Nicholas, then it would only be a matter of a short space of time before he could make himself the official boyfriend and everything would be there for the taking, or at least for the asking. Chuckling like a child given an un-expected bag of his favourite sweets Jim resumed his journey.

There were no doubts in his head now that once she was shot of pompous Nicholas Page Maura would become his partner and he would be made for life. The thought that had come into his mind when he first saw the grown-up Maura resurfaced: that he could do a lot worse than marry or shack up with his cousin. He must get his version of what happened when he applied for a job with Nicholas Page enterprises to her as soon as possible. His astute brain raced along, concocting the story he would tell to this rather delectable and certainly desirable cousin. It should be simple to put himself in a good light and paint the other man as a villain.

As for the further thought that once rid of Page he would sweep her off her feet, as the heroes always did in the old movies, it would be a piece of cake. He had that fraudulent scrapbook of 'his' grand place in Canada with him here. What a good job he had put it in; it certainly wouldn't be the first time it had come in very very useful. He would stress that there was no blood relationship between them, that 'dear old Tom' as he always referred to his stepfather, and he had got on very well indeed, and that he was very glad that his dear mother had married the man 'who treated me as his own son.' Yes, he had his act off to perfection. The only thing wrong was that 'dear old Tom' had left his niece everything and cut him out completely.

His mind worked rapidly. He *must* see Maura and tell her that he had only applied for a job at the restaurant so as not to eat into his capital too rapidly now he had decided to extend his holiday for a while. He would be suitably sad and angry at the same time and, when pressed, would hint at first, and then tell her outright of some of the dreadful things Nicholas Page said about her. Awful unrepeatable things. 'I wouldn't tell you, but if - well, if you're going to marry this man I think you should know what he is really like. It hurts me to do it, cuz,' he'd say quietly, 'but best surely to know now rather than find out when it's too late.

'I stood up for you of course,' he would add. 'Said that although I hadn't seen or known you since you were little I was a good judge of people and I know you are not the sort of girl he indicated at all.' He would finish by telling her that he wouldn't work for that man now if he begged him on his hands and knees. 'Not after the way he rubbished you, cuz, no way.'

Jim was supremely confident that he could bring this off. His greatest difficulty was how to do it. He needed to see her face to face and convince her, and he had to do so before that clot got in with his story. He could waylay her when she left the Escudo building tonight. If she was there. That was the problem, because often she was out modelling somewhere else. The other way would be to wait outside her flat, but if she didn't come straight home precious time would be lost and it was vital to get his story in first. In the end he decided to wait outside Escudo's – there was always someone there, and if she didn't come out, then to go to her flat. If she wasn't there he would leave a note marked urgent for her to contact him at Doris's. Yes, that would be best. He carried on with a lighter step. Picton Manor, I'm on my way, the rhythm in his steps seemed to be saying to him as he hurried along the busy streets.

'That bloody cousin of yours is trying to get on the bandwagon of our success, Maura,' Nicholas said later that evening when they were sharing a late night drink in his flat.

'What, Jim from Canada?'

'Of course. How many cousins have you got over here?'

Her thoughts had been wandering, as they so often did these days, to Ross. Picturing him back there in his home in Picton, working on the farmland which he loved...

'Maura?'

'Sorry, Nick. My mind was far away. How is Jim trying to get on the bandwagon?'

'He applied for a job and then turned up harassing me and the staff. He's a menace and I don't trust him.'

'Don't trust him, Nick? In what way? Do you think he would steal from you?'

'Wouldn't put it past him. He seems a dodgy character to me. Bit of a con man. Not sure what he's after, though.'

'The manor house, Nick. He thinks it should have been left to him instead of me. In fact he told me there was another, later will, actually leaving it to him.'

Nick looked at her sharply. 'Yes, I remember you said. You don't believe that, do you?'

'Of course I don't. The solicitor would have known about it, but from the little I know about Jim I gather he has always been a bit of a dreamer.'

'Like I said, a con man. Well, he's not getting his feet under the table here nor at Picton. The sooner he realizes this and goes back to Canada the better. Now, about our trip down there – the manager's off at Nick's Place this weekend – family wedding in Scotland, would you believe. It is his weekend off anyway, and the wedding was planned around that. I must admit I'd forgotten when I said we'd go this weekend, so let's make it in the week instead.'

'Sorry, I've a full week of engagements. Only Wednesday afternoon free, and that is no use for our purpose. I'll go while I have the chance at the weekend. I can check on everything and you can go down next week while I'm working if you need to.'

Nick swore mildly, then grinned at her. 'I guess that's what it'll have to be. Blooming nuisance, though, I was hoping for a lovely weekend there with you.'

Chapter 25

Maura drove down to Picton early on Friday afternoon. She read the pathetic little note Jim had left at Escudo's for her, then tore it up and threw it in the bin. Back at the flat she packed a small case and made her way to the car park at the back of the flats. As she drove round the corner and on to the road she thought the figure striding along from the direction of the station looked liked Jim Wareham. She couldn't be sure from that distance, but she heaved a sigh of relief that, if it was, she had escaped him. He was becoming a real pain.

The Friday afternoon traffic was heavy and the journey took longer than usual, but Mrs Duffy's welcome took away her niggling worries about cousin Jim who had erupted into her life recently. Although she didn't go along completely with Nick's assessment that he was a con man, she did think he was putting on an act to acquire some of her legacy. She didn't believe there was another will but she did think that he had only come over to see what he could get from the family estate.

'It's good to be back,' she said to the smiling housekeeper. 'Nicholas will probably be down for a couple of days during next week but I'll let you know which ones when we know ourselves. He couldn't get away this weekend and I'm working most of next week.'

'Thank you, miss. What time would you like to eat this evening?'

'Whenever it suits you, Mrs D,' she said, unconsciously using Ross's abbreviation of the name. 'If we have it early you'll have more of an evening for yourself. Just tell me when to come down. I'll be doing some sorting of books and bits and pieces, I think, and tomorrow I'll get something to eat while I'm out because I'll be dashing around the district a bit. I'll be returning to London late Sunday afternoon.'

Upstairs in her bedroom she stood by the window for a few minutes looking down into the rose garden. Would she see Ross while she was here? She felt her muscles quiver and tighten at the thought, then common sense took over and she knew she would not seek him out, because of Jane. If he came over it was a different scenario. She felt happier with herself now that she had decided that she was not going to marry Nick. A business partnership was fine. She was fond of him and in the life she led in London they had so much in common. Their friends thought of them as a pair and seldom invited one without the other. This was such a far cry from her overwhelming feelings when she was with Ross, but because Nick wanted the Manor Restaurant so badly she knew he would eventually agree to a business partnership only. He had surprised her when he had produced that gorgeous ring but the thought of being committed for the rest of her life was frightening. Not because she wasn't fond of Nick – she was, but even before Ross had re-entered her life she had doubts about a permanent partnership with him. She had always thought that when and if she married it would be for life. Fine to play the field before but divorce simply because she had mated with the wrong man was not on the cards for her. She remembered a conversation she'd had with another model who was leaving to be married some time ago. 'If it doesn't work out I can get a divorce after a couple of years,' she had said.

Maybe I'm old-fashioned, Maura thought now, but that's the way it is. Or perhaps it's simply that I cannot bear to fail at anything. She remembered saying to the bride-to-be, 'But you're in love with him, aren't you?'

'Yes, of course,' the other girl replied, 'but that's no guarantee, is it? I've been in love before but it wears off after a while.' Then she added, grinning and tweaking Maura's cheek, 'Anyway, he may fall out of love with me – it works both ways, you know. We shall give it a go and see what happens.'

Turning away from the window now Maura thought that if only she had the money she would not be considering anything for the manor house except to live in it. She needed Nicholas Page's input to keep her home and she had no doubts in her mind that this would turn out to be one of the best restaurants in the whole of Wiltshire. Even in the whole of the southern part of England. What was it Nick had compared it to, the cuisine Glyndebourne of England? The Rolls Royce of restaurants? Well, maybe. She would still rather it was her home and sanctuary but without his

267

commitment she would definitely have to sell and that prospect was worse than sharing part of it with the public for a while.

With dinner safely cooking in the oven and the gas heating the saucepans on the top of the stove turned down to a glimmer Mrs Duffy switched her little radio on and went into the hall to use the telephone there. She looked guiltily up the stairs, hoping Maura's bedroom door was closed and that the voices and music from the radio would mask her own devious activity. With her hand shaking slightly she rang the number Ross Edwards had given her.

To her relief he answered swiftly and she told him that Maura was home and that she was alone.

'Thanks, Mrs D and God bless you.'

She found she was still trembling when she replaced the receiver. She hurried back to her kitchen.

Maura had just finished her meal when Ross telephoned.

'Oh good, you are there,' he said amiably, 'I thought it was your car I saw turning into the lane as I went by earlier this afternoon. I've been given two tickets for the theatre in Salisbury Saturday evening. Would you like to come? They're doing–'

Taken aback, Maura said, 'Why me, Ross?'

'Why not you?' he replied easily. 'As I recall you always enjoyed a trip to the theatre. How about it, Maura?'

After a bit of banter, during which she just managed to refrain from asking why he hadn't asked Jane to accompany him, she agreed that he could call for her at 6.30 the following day and that they would simply have a snack beforehand and eat properly when they came home from the show.

Saturday morning was taken up with visits to the builder's office and checking dates for the start of the alterations. Thumbing through his orders book the manager said, 'I'll put it down for the second week in August for the kitchen. The plumber will do a two-toilet block in the entrance, he's down to do that the first week in August, so it should be finished by the time we start on the kitchen. All the essential services are there. I have the contract in my office and once you have both signed it I'll get the project under way. Half the money when you sign and the rest when the job is completed to your satisfaction.' He closed the book and stood up. 'And tell that chap of yours we'll have you ready to open your restaurant in September, never fear.'

That evening, driving into Salisbury, she told Ross that everything was set now and the alterations would begin in August. 'Only the kitchen and a couple of loos in the entrance hall,' she said, 'because we are leaving the drawing and dining room as they are. Well, we shall take the furniture out, of course, and fill it with tables and chairs, but no structural stuff there.'

'And the library?'

'Will stay as it is.' She turned to smile at him. 'I fought hard for that, and Uncle Tom's study. We will probably use the study for a small office, but no walls are coming down.'

'Good.' Ross's voice was brisk. 'You shouldn't have to fight for it, Maura, it's your property after all.'

'The property, yes, but the money to turn it into a swish restaurant is coming from Nick. And before you say anything Ross, I couldn't keep it on without that.'

Chapter 26

Back in London on Sunday evening there was a message from Esmeralda to say she had some exciting news and when could they meet. Maura phoned her and learned that a small independent company was keen to make a series of films about various jobs and she was to be in at least three of them. 'One as a model, showing the ups and downs of that career, and the script is good,' she said. 'Well, I did have a little input into that and the writer listened because he knew that modelling had been part of my life. Then there's to be one about a musician. I do play the violin and piano and can strum a bit on the guitar, so I'm to be doing that one too.'

'That's great news, Esmeralda,' Maura said. 'What's the third one?'

'Management. It's another great script; they're all by the same writer, incidentally, and he's not only good but he's dishy too. They wanted to show girls that a career in management can be interesting and fulfilling. I get to wear some classic outfits in that one, and that alone makes you feel powerful, you know. We start filming in a couple of weeks, so perhaps we can meet up before I become embroiled in masses of work?'

'I'll check my free time when I go in tomorrow and give you a buzz,' Maura said.

The manager at Nick's Place had an accident and was in hospital for a few days. As they already had one waiter off sick and one on holiday Nick went along there and couldn't get down to Picton during the week after all. 'Never mind, if you're free at the weekend we can both go down and one of us stay on to supervise the work. At least we are nearly under way,' Nick said philosophically.

Maura rang Esmeralda and they met for a light lunch in between two of Maura's assignments. The former model was excited about her new role as an actress. 'Not quite Hollywood yet, but it will be interesting, I shall be paid and it could lead to other things.'

They talked about Escudo but Maura didn't mention the advances Craig had made. Instead she said, 'When you have finished your film-making and have a spare day or weekend perhaps you could come down to the manor with me. We should have the restaurant going by then and–'

'Hey, we might even be able to use your manor house and grounds for background for some films, Maura. It's quite a small company but I think it will do well. They could hire the manor for a day for filming and that would bring you in some money and give them a marvellous country-house setting. They have several small films and documentaries in mind, I know, and one is a short costume drama set in a country house. What do you think?'

'Well, we could talk about it later. Once we've got the restaurant under way. We are hoping to open at the end of September, but I'll know more once the builders have got started. It's going to have a new kitchen suitable for a restaurant and a set of ladies' and gents' in the entrance hall. The kitchen will take the longest time to do.'

Esmeralda was positively bubbling over with excitement now. 'I've just had a wonderful idea, Maura. How about a Christmas film? A love story beginning with two people who meet in your restaurant and are marooned in the snow at Christmas time and–'

Maura giggled, 'Not so fast,' she said, 'it isn't even open yet. You sound just like Nick, he can see possibilities long before they happen.'

'I guess you're right. Sometimes my imagination runs riot, but there's the germ of an idea there, isn't there?'

Maura nodded her head. 'Yes, probably is. Once we're rolling we can talk about it. It isn't something I've thought about, hiring the manor out, but I can't see anything against it. Your people would simply come along and film for a day, I suppose.' She stood up and hugged her friend. 'I must fly, I've got a date with a collection of hats, handbags and gloves. I'll be in touch.'

Before she left Escudo's later she checked her schedule for the following week. There were three clear days, Monday, Tuesday and Wednesday.

Some of the girls were getting changed from a small wedding display which had been held in the downstairs salon. Among them was a slender copper-haired beauty who looked no more than eighteen.

'Craig brought her in this afternoon,' one of the girls whispered to Maura. 'His latest acquisition, I think.' Among themselves most of the girls used his first name.

Maura pondered the situation as she made her way home. Perhaps now would be a good time to get out. Although she took other work apart from Escudo's, he was her

274

main source of income and it seemed as though that could be drying up, in spite of his words of reassurance after her refusal to become involved in his private life. Time to have a serious talk with her agent, she thought.

Nick rang to say that he was fully staffed again and could get away on Friday for the weekend. 'I'll probably return to London on Sunday night or Monday morning, Maura, and come back Wednesday or Thursday. How are you fixed for next week? Once we've signed that contract work could go ahead and one or other of us will be there most of the time to check it out.'

'At the moment I'm clear until Thursday, Nick,' she said.

'Good girl. I knew you would manage it. We'll go down this Friday, then. It couldn't be better.' He chattered on for a few moments before saying, 'You all right, Maura? You seem very quiet.'

'I'm fine. A little tired, that's all.'

'The country air will soon put that right. By the way, Anne and Pete are back from holiday so I've updated them on our latest project and they're going to spread the word. There'll be no lack of diners from London, darling. In fact I think we could

275

make it a feature of the advertising. The fact that it is *out* of London. There is a smallish restaurant in Sussex, somewhere on the Downs, it is, and people regularly go there with their friends. It's not cheap but it is special. I believe even the Queen goes there sometimes.'

They drove to Picton late Friday afternoon. They travelled in separate cars because she was staying on for the extra few days, 'and I shall need wheels,' she said. Her spirits lifted a trifle when they went over the bridge, Nick driving much too fast as usual. They rose even more when the manor house came into her sights.

On Monday the arrangements would be finalized and work could start the following week. Mrs Duffy would be there when Maura returned to London on Wednesday night and even Nick was happy about that. 'One of us can always get down in a few hours should anything urgent crop up,' he had said the previous evening, 'and she's had it cushy since your uncle died anyway.'

Nick left just after ten on Monday morning. The sky was beautiful with clouds like pure white castles painted on to a blue background. It lifted her spirits just to look at it. Maura loved the sky in most of its moods, but Nick carried his black leather case to the car without glancing upwards. He deposited it on the passenger seat, then turned to her.

'I'll ring you this evening, Maura, and I'll see you on Wednesday after your stint with the plumbers. Once that's done we can get on with the kitchen.' He put his arms round her. 'Getting excited, darling?' Without waiting for an answer he went on, 'I am. Although it's a fourth time for me it's still a thrill when you see your plans taking shape. We are being very, very modest to start with, but you know, I fancy that might even be the right approach for this place. Let it happen gradually and the locals and people from all over the country will soon be flocking here in their hundreds. I'm placing adverts in all the strategic places and telling the right people about it. We shall probably have a crowd of celebrities at the opening.' He kissed her. 'I'll phone before you go to bed tonight, sweetie.' Then he was in the car and racing down the drive.

He was at the end of the drive when another car turned in. Maura heard it coming and turned round to see who it was.

'What a lovely morning,' Ross said cheerfully as he leapt out and came towards her. 'I thought Nicholas was only here until Sunday. That was him shooting out just now, wasn't it?'

She nodded and her body immediately responded to Ross's nearness.

'I'm more used to the kitchen entrance than the front door,' Ross said. 'Better take my boots off.'

Mrs Duffy came through the hall at that moment. She bestowed a huge smile in Ross's direction as she wished him good morning. As he turned to close the door another car roared up. There was a squeal of brakes, the car door slammed and Nicholas Page strode towards the group framed in the still open doorway. Ross had one boot on and the other half on and half off.

'All very cosy. Couldn't even wait until I was out of the village.' Nick went straight for Maura and swung her towards him. 'No wonder you were so anxious to see the back of me,' he shouted. 'Not very clever to fix your next assignment so early, was it? Or did you have to be sandwiched in between milking the cows and mucking out the pigs? Well, I've caught you now and—'

'Don't you talk like that to Maura.' Ross grabbed Nick's arm and pulled him outside,

278

kicking off the remaining boot as he went.

Nick's fist shot out, catching Ross on the chin. The next minute the two men were embroiled in fisticuffs while Maura rushed outside, begging them to stop. Although Nick was the bigger man Ross was fitter but his lack of shoes hampered him. Nick went for his opponent's face but after the first connecting blow Ross weaved and dodged, all the while getting in some punches to the other man's chest.

Maura moved as the two men circled each other, to try to separate them, but Mrs Duffy pulled her back. Nick got in another blow to Ross's face and they saw a trickle of blood seeping from his lip when suddenly a left hook from Ross sent Nick spinning round and panting for breath.

Ross stopped immediately and went to the other man's aid as he almost collapsed against the fence. Maura and Mrs Duffy rushed over and with Ross's help got Nick indoors and into the big old armchair which lived in the kitchen. Ross ran his hands gently but expertly over his opponent.

'Nothing broken,' he said, relief in his voice. 'More winded than anything else I think.'

Maura fetched some water and Mrs Duffy put the kettle on. It was five minutes before

Nick was able to speak and when he did it was to Ross. 'Get out,' he said.

Ross looked at Maura. 'You know where I am should you want me, Maura.'

'Your lip, Ross. Let me bathe it for you.'

He rubbed his hand against the rapidly congealing blood at the corner of his mouth. 'I'll do it at home.' Silently he went for his shoes and left.

Nicholas Page did not return to London that day and although Mrs Duffy said privately to Maura that she thought his pride was more hurt than he was, Maura was worried. She longed to go after Ross too, but she couldn't see him allowing her to make a fuss of him. He would bathe his lip and then get on with whatever he had planned to do before the fracas.

She rang Primrose Cottage later after she had put some balm on Nick's bruises and he had gone to sleep. There was no reply so she busied herself with lists and sorting. She could see how it must have appeared from Nick's point of view, but her heart was full when she thought of Ross's swift defence of her. Later she decided she would walk to the cottage to check that his lip was OK. A sharp stab of pain shot through her body at the thought that Jane had probably administered first aid to him.

Although her decision had already been made she was more sure than ever that she could never marry Nick – not because of the fight but because she still loved Ross. She would sell the manor and return to her flat and her modelling work for a while and then maybe she could find a job abroad.

The ringing of the telephone startled her. It was Jane. 'Ross asked me to speak to you in case you were not alone. He wants to know if you are all right, Maura,' she said in a quiet voice.

'I'm fine, thank you, Jane. How is Ross?'

'He's OK. Sticking with cold drinks and soft food for today because of his sore lip, but he'll do.'

Suddenly Ross's voice came over the line. 'Don't be too proud to ask for help if you need to, Maura. I promise I won't interfere but I'm here for you always – remember that.'

She heard the door open in the other room and realized that the telephone had woken Nick. 'Thank you both,' she said before turning her attention to a petulant-looking Nicholas.

'The deal about the restaurant is off,' she told Nick that evening. 'I shall sell the manor.'

'And us, Maura? I can find another restaurant but you and I are good together.'

She shook her head. 'We were,' she acknowledged, 'but we were an interlude, I think. We want, we *need*, different things from life. I see that now. I'm truly sorry, Nick.'

Chapter 27

Jim walked purposefully towards the restaurant, one hand in his pocket where he could feel the new box of matches which would light the first flame towards recovering his inheritance. He had done his homework and knew from talking to the manager of Nick's Place, the middle one of the three establishments, that Nicholas Page would not be in his flat above the more flamboyant Nick's Palace in the West End.

'Need a job over here for a few months,' Jim had told him, 'and I've done relief manager work in this trade before.'

'Best to write in the first place.'

'I've done that and Mr Page said to call in and make an appointment sometime, but Nick's Palace is always so busy and I don't want to scupper my chance by being a nuisance and calling at the wrong time.'

'Beginning of the week's usually best to catch him, but he's not there this Monday and Tuesday, I know. He's at a food convention up north. I'm going when he comes back.'

'Thanks. I'll leave it a few more days then.'

Although he had cultivated a sort of friendship with the Nick's Place manager this was luckier than he had expected. To know that the flat above the restaurant would be empty for two days was a real bonus.

As long as I'm not seen immediately afterwards, he thought, everything will be fine. I'll be on a train to Wiltshire before the blaze has really taken hold. I'll be roaming over the manor by the time the police want to interview me. Then again I might be back in London, but with an established alibi because that stupid old housekeeper will vouchsafe that I was indeed sitting in her kitchen and drinking a cup of tea that morning.

He was wearing an old pair of trousers, a black shirt, dark plimsolls and carrying a khaki-coloured haversack. He retrieved a crate which he had found and carefully hidden behind one of the garages a little further

283

along. After a quick look around the area behind Nick's Palace, he put it beneath the window of the toilets. The window wasn't high and he could have reached without the crate but he needed it to give himself enough leverage to climb inside. He had his story ready should anyone come round – that someone was trapped and had been calling for help before he heard a crash and a scream. He was trying to get in to rescue whoever it was and had already called the police on his mobile.

The silence was eerie, yet comforting because it ensured he would easily pick up the slightest sound. Standing on his box he took from the haversack some duct tape and a small jar of honey. Liberally smearing the honey over the entire window with a rag that he pulled from his pocket, he attached the tape, and from his other pocket he took out a diamond cutter. This was a trick he had learned from a regular burglar and in a matter of moments he had silently taken the glass out and was getting himself down to ground level. He propped the glass up against the brick wall of the building. Another five seconds and he was back on the crate and climbing through the gap, into the gent's lavatory.

Jim lit the corners of all the tablecloths, moving swiftly and methodically from the front of the restaurant to the back. He took a lightly oiled rag from the zipped pocket of the haversack and rubbed it over the centre of each table before returning to the gents and hoisting himself up and through the gap once more. He pushed the rag into a plastic bag, replaced it in the side of the haversack and walked round the corner away from the scene.

He hurried down the street, not running but walking fast. He turned into Oxford Circus underground station, bought a ticket to Waterloo from the machine and caught the tube within five minutes. He doubted if the place was on fire yet, and was glad. The tablecloths were cotton damask and would smoulder for quite a while, but with luck it wouldn't be noticed until they were blazing and the flames had caught the furniture. The longer it took the further away he would be. No one would be going into the building for several hours yet, and by the time the fire was discovered and put out, thousands of pounds worth of damage could be done.

He caught the Salisbury train with half a minute to spare, having bought his ticket the day before to save time and to avoid detection should the ticket office staff at the station be questioned about anybody purchasing one that morning. He had pulled off his gloves which would have looked out of place should he meet anyone, but he was in a sort of disguise. A short-haired dark wig concealed his blonde hair and sunglasses were in his shirt pocket in case he needed a new appearance quickly. He settled into a seat, closed his eyes, but kept hold of the haversack, letting it rest loosely on his lap but with his arm through the strap.

He travelled in his old clothes and swapped them in the gents at Salisbury station for the shorts and bright-blue T-shirt he had in the haversack. He rammed the wig in too, and set off to walk to the manor. It was a little over two and a half miles and the weather was perfect for such a jaunt, he thought. As he swung along, munching on the cheese roll he had brought with him, he went over in his mind what he was going to say to account for his presence in the area. He knew Mrs Duffy was still there. She must be getting on in years now, he thought, but at least she will know who I am, whereas a newer house-keeper might not let me in.

It would be good to see the old place again

and assess its possibilities. A restaurant wouldn't have been the first thing that came to his mind, but Maura's boyfriend had certainly proved himself so far with his businesses in that line. He could turn the upstairs into a spacious flat for himself, always have access to food without the bother of cooking it and, more important, have rent coming in regularly. With the type of restaurant Nicholas Page seemed to be planning it would be an all-year-round income too. The prospects looked even better than he had imagined when he came over, but he had to play his cards right.

When Mrs Duffy opened the heavy front door she did not recognize the man who stood there smiling at her.

'It's Mrs Duffy, isn't it? How lovely to see you again.' He thrust his hand towards her. 'Jim from Canada, back in the old country for a few months and on a nostalgic trip to see the homestead again. I was so sorry when my stepdad died. Wish I could have got here for the funeral but I was heavily committed over there and couldn't get away. This is the first chance I've had since.'

Mrs Duffy was staring hard at him. 'We haven't seen you for a long, long time,' she said slowly, 'but I suppose you had better come in for a few minutes.' Her inbuilt sense of hospitality made her add, 'Expect you could do with a drink, I'll put the kettle on.'

Ensconced in the kitchen with a mug of tea and a piece of home-made fruitcake Jim breathed freely again. He wasn't sure just how much the housekeeper knew but he was in now and well away from the events of the early hours. As long as he kept his haversack holding the incriminating evidence of his dawn activities with him until he returned to London he was in the clear. No one could prove or disprove how long he had been in the area and he could get rid of the oily rag later in a bin somewhere back in the capital.

'Miss Maura isn't at home just now.' Mrs Duffy's voice sounded strained. 'She won't be here until the weekend.'

'I know, Mrs Duffy. I saw her last week in London. My, she is doing well, isn't she? She's a lovely girl. I hadn't seen her for ages of course, although I met Tom at his club the last time I was over. He invited me down here then but I had a lot of business to do in town and a deadline for my return to Canada, so I couldn't make it. Who would have thought that when I eventually did, he would be gone?'

Mrs Duffy was saved from answering because there was a sharp rap on the back door and she hurried to see who it was. Ross Edwards was standing there with half a dozen brown eggs in a bowl.

'Couldn't be fresher,' he said, handing them over. 'Still warm when I picked them up. Enjoy them.'

As he turned to leave she put her hand on his arm. 'Please come in. I've just made a fresh pot of tea for us.'

The pleading look she gave him and her rather strange manner bothered him. He didn't really have time to linger this morning – had simply stopped by with the fresh eggs because he knew she liked to give some to her daughter. However, she seemed so ill at ease that he followed her into the kitchen.

'This is Maura's cousin Jim,' she said to him. 'He's over from Canada.'

Jim held out his hand but Ross ignored it as he pulled out a sturdy wooden chair and sat down.

'So what are you doing here, Jim?' he said quietly.

'Bit of business and a bit of a holiday.'

'Where are you staying?'

Jim was ready for that one and although he privately thought it was none of Ross's business he answered him civilly enough. 'With a mate in Warminster. He had to go to work so I caught an early train over here to see the place again.'

'Does Maura know you're here?'

'Yes, she does. I spent the evening with her a few days ago. Not that it's got anything to do with you. You were always hanging round here in the old days, I remember, but there's nothing in it for you, mate. The manor stays in the family and that's Maura and me.'

Ross turned to Mrs Duffy, 'I'll pop back later, Mrs D,' he said, 'when you haven't any other visitors.' Her look of appeal wasn't lost on him and with a perfunctory nod to Jim he took his leave and headed home quickly. Hastily he looked on his pad for the telephone number and was relieved when he heard the house-keeper's warm voice at the other end.

'Mrs D. Would you like me to phone Maura and tell her Jim is there?' he said quietly into the receiver.

'Yes, please.'

'I don't want to interfere,' Ross went on, his voice only one decibel above a whisper, 'and I don't know how much you are aware of past relations between Jim and his step-father, but I know he was not welcome at the manor. I'm wondering what has suddenly brought him here.'

'Me too,' she said. 'But if you do what you suggest that will be good and a load off my mind. I'm a bit busy at the moment, you see.'

'Yes, I do and I understand perfectly. I'll pop back later when I've done it to see how you're getting on. With getting rid of him,' he added, in a real whisper this time.

Mrs Duffy returned to the kitchen. 'Nice bit of cake,' Jim said. 'Like my dear old mum used to make. Now don't let me disturb you, I'll just have a nostalgic nosy around the old place, then I'll have to get off because I've a bit of business to do in Salisbury and I promised my pal I'd be back in time to go for a drink with him and some of his mates in Warminster tonight.'

He swung the haversack on to his shoulder and walked across to the kitchen door. 'I'll give a shout when I'm going,' he said, 'and I'll be down again with Maura before I go back to Canada anyway, but a quick look around the grounds before I go off walking will be great. It's a long while since I saw them, you know.'

Mrs Duffy watched from the kitchen window as he sauntered along the path by the herb garden, through the arch until he was lost to sight. She hadn't seen Jim for years and although she didn't know what it had been about she did know there had been a family row concerning him. She felt uneasy that he was now roaming around the place. Well, there's nothing he can steal from the garden, she thought. The two old urns were far too large and heavy to fit into that haversack he had with him and there were no valuable statues or bronzes or anything like that. She walked back to the table and poured herself another cup of tea.

Meanwhile Jim wandered about, turning to look at the building from various viewpoints as he refreshed his memories of the manor house. Hmm, not bad, not bad at all. At least it isn't crumbling to pieces, and obviously the old boy would have left some money with it. Money and property which should rightfully belong to me because, after all, he did marry my mother, Jim thought bitterly. I'm his stepson and that hoity-toity girl Maura is only his niece. His sister's child while I am his wife's child. Of course I would win if I took her to court to claim – no doubt about it. But it would cost and I haven't got a bean at present. The only way is to marry her myself or to cajole her into giving me my share.

So engrossed was he that he didn't hear Mrs Duffy come round behind him and when she spoke he whipped round so fast he almost knocked her over.

'Afraid you'll have to go now,' she said. 'I'm expecting the builders today and I'll be busy on Miss Maura's behalf. All the power will be off for several hours so I can't cook anything but I'll tell her you called when she phones me this evening.'

Jim opened his mouth, then changed his mind, deciding to play along and make the most of the situation to further his cause. 'That's fine by me,' he said, 'but I couldn't go walking in this area without popping in to see the old place and this was the only chance I had for a while. I'll be back when Maura's down again, but I'll get out of your way now and let you get on. Thanks for the tea and cake.' He walked round the corner of the manor and went down the front drive whistling *Home, Sweet Home.*

Chapter 28

Nicholas Page drove back to London early on Tuesday morning after the police had been in touch with him about the fire. He stood on the pavement and looked at the mess inside Nick's Palace, then he rang Maura. 'They won't let me in at present, the fire engines are still here and apparently everything is being assessed, but the structure is OK they tell me. So thank heavens for that. And for the smoke alarm,' he added.

'Was anyone hurt, Nick?'

'No, it happened when the place was shut. Arson. Someone got in through the small window in the gents. Cut the glass out very neatly, smearing it with something sticky first so it didn't fall and make a noise. It was a professional at work here, Maura.'

She heard the catch in his voice and said, 'I'll come over. I have a session later this morning so I'll bring my things with me and see you as soon as I can make it. OK, Nick?'

'No, wait. I can't get into my flat yet; goodness knows when they'll let me. In fact

294

I don't think there's much else I can do here and the police want me to go to the station with them and make a statement, so how about I come over to you when I can get away. What time is your session?'

'Twelve o'clock.'

'Right, if I *can't* get to the flat before you leave I'll get a message to you at Escudo's. Meanwhile I think there's a lot of red tape to sort out here as well as clearing up the place once I'm allowed inside.'

The fire at Nick's Palace made the national papers. Not front page news but featured prominently inside and when Maura rang Ross the following day to thank him for alerting her to Jim's visit to the manor, Ross said, 'Is there much damage to Nicholas Page's place?'

'Several thousand pounds' worth, but the building is fine. No structural damage. It will take a while to get it cleaned up and re-painted, and it will need new furniture and table linen.'

'Have they any idea who was responsible, Maura?'

'I don't think so, although they had Nick at the station for several hours questioning him. He is insured, obviously, but he said they were taking the line that he could have driven down from the north during the night and let himself in with his key and set fire to the tablecloths himself for the insurance money.'

'And the window?'

'That he did that too, to make it look like an intruder. But Ross, Nick wouldn't do that and in any case the place was making money. He isn't in any kind of financial trouble with any of the restaurants. It's crazy.'

'I agree with you,' Ross said quietly. 'I obviously have no liking for him but I don't think he would do that, either. So what is going to happen about the manor restaurant?'

'The deal is off. I told Nick after that last visit to Picton that I was pulling out. I shall probably sell the manor house now.'

In the silence she could hear Ross's breath close to the phone.

'Please don't do anything until we've talked, Maura. *Please*. It's not something we can say over the phone so when are you coming down? Or can I come up and see you?'

'I *was* coming down later this week. I've no sessions lined up for two days, but I must stay here now and help Nick get the Palace back on line. There will be a great deal to

296

do, making good, painting, buying new furniture and tablecloths,' her voice caught on a sob.

'You are staying up there with Nicholas Page, then?' he said quietly.

'No, Ross, I'm not. Not permanently that is, but I simply cannot leave him in this mess. I've helped him with this business for several years now – oh, I've not been key to it but I do know what it's all about and I can't abandon a friend and leave him in this wilderness. He said he thought the police were actually going to arrest and charge him with arson, even though he is totally innocent.'

'He's lucky he has you as a friend, Maura.'

'You would do the same,' she said quietly. 'You rang to tell me about Jim's visit to the manor. He isn't still hanging around, is he?'

'No. Apparently he left to go walking, then back to his pals in Warminster the same day. He said that you were going to have him down next time you were there, Maura. Is that true or was he indulging in one of his daydreams? He always used to.'

'I don't recall issuing any invitation. I get the feeling that once he has his feet under the table I would never shift him.'

Ross rang her back ten minutes later.

'Maura, I suddenly remembered an envelope Tom gave me some years ago. He told me to open it only if, when he was gone, Jim gave you any trouble regarding the manor. I'd actually forgotten it until now, but, well, do you want me to check it out?'

'Oh Ross, I – I don't know. It seems strange, doesn't it? To give it to you, I mean. If it was anything legal surely the solicitor would have it?'

'Maybe, but, well, he gave it to me as I was leaving one evening. We had been playing chess, I remember, and he suddenly said, "I want you to do something for me if you will Ross". He took this envelope from the mantelpiece and handed it to me. "Not to be opened until and unless it is necessary you understand, Ross", he said. "But if, when I've gone to pastures new Jim tries to make trouble, as he well might, then please open it and do whatever is necessary. Will you do this for me, please?" I can picture it as clearly as if it were yesterday, yet I had forgotten completely about it until a few moments ago.'

She was silent for a moment and Ross said, 'I can't get up to London until this evening, but I could bring it up then and you can open it, Maura. Tom obviously suspected that Jim might interfere when he left you the manor. Your uncle was a meticulous man and we know your cousin is furious about being left out of his will.'

'You open it, Ross. It might even be this other will that Jim is on about.'

'I doubt that. I'll bring the letter up this evening and we can look at it together. Shall I come to your flat? Or we could have a meal together at a restaurant or pub close to the station because I shall need to go home tonight.'

'All right, Ross. Let me know which train you'll be on and I'll be at the barrier waiting.'

They went to a small Italian restaurant not far from the station and chose a table for two in a corner at the back, well away from most of the noise. Ross handed her the envelope and it gave her a strange feeling to see her uncle's once familiar handwriting again. They checked the menu and gave their order. Then Ross said, 'Better open it so we can discuss whatever it contains, Maura.' He had almost said *darling* but looking at her tense expression had kept it totally business like.

She used the small outside knife to slit the narrow envelope, then drew out an A4 sheet of paper which was folded into three. It was typed and began *Dear Ross...* Quickly handing it over she said, 'You read it, it's addressed to you.'

'You sure?' She nodded, and passed the letter over. Ross read it in silence and without any strong expression on his face. When he had finished he handed it to her. 'You had better read it, Maura, and then I'll do what Tom asked and sort it out.'

Jim Wareham became my stepson when I married his mother. He was twelve years old then and already out of hand. I tried, I really tried with him but he was a selfish and self-centred child who had had his own way for many years. If he did not get it he did drastic things. Twice he almost set light to our home, he regularly stole money from his mother and tried to blame others and as he grew to manhood he became adept at what he called his S. Schemes. It was several years before I found out the S was for swindling. He would gloat about them, how he had conned people into giving him money and, on one occasion at least, property. Twice during all this I reported him to the police but there was never enough evidence to convict him. After the second occasion I banned him from the manor and told him never to come back. We had a huge row and apart from some vindictive and extremely threatening letters there has been no communication between us for years. I am telling you all this, Ross, because you are like a son to me and I am asking you to protect Maura when Jim learns (as he will) that I have left her the manor house. You will only be reading this if he tries to make trouble. I have the will watertight but I know Jim pretty well and he will stop at nothing to gain possession of anything he wants. He is a passable forger, a good liar and a thief. He uses charm (yes, he can be charming) and any underhand method to gain his way and once he has set his sights on something he really does go to drastic lengths to get what he wants. Below is a list of scams I am sure he was behind, including the two I went to the police about. I should have gone to the police right at the start but I didn't because of his mother. I am sorry to put all this on to you, Ross, but I need someone to look out for my beloved Maura when I am gone and I know you love her too and will defend her against Jim whatever happens between Maura and yourself. God bless you, Ross. Be happy and thank you, Tom. (Tom Wareham)

Their food arrived as she reached the bottom of the page and when the waiter had gone she looked across the table at Ross.

'It's awful, isn't it? How could he? I mean, it must have been he who started the fire at Nick's Palace, mustn't it?'

'I'm afraid so, my love. He's a bad egg and has always had his sights on the main chance. He must have caught a very early train to Salisbury to give himself an alibi. He didn't expect me to turn up but when I did it gave him two witnesses to prove he was in Wiltshire and not London. Clever and underhand, but he'll find he's bitten off more than he can chew this time.'

'What can you do, Ross? There isn't any proof it was Jim who torched Nick's Palace.'

'There isn't any proof that it wasn't either. If I show the police this letter they will be able to trace his movements He managed to get from London to Picton early in the morning. How? Did he hitch a lift? Did a friend drive him some of the way? Did he come by train or coach to Salisbury and walk. He said he came from Warminster where he was staying with a friend. All this can be checked, especially if he thinks he has got away with it. Where is he staying in London?'

'I don't know. He said with an old mate, but didn't say where.'

'Did he mention the mate's name, Maura?'

'No. Oh, wait a minute, Ross, he took me to a friend's place once. It was a café in a back street, well behind Oxford Street. I could probably find it again. But I don't think he was staying there. He introduced the woman who was running the place as a friend of his. What did he say her name was ... oh no, I've forgotten. Damn.'

'Never mind, you could find this place again, could you?'

'I'm sure I could.'

'Will you leave it with me at the moment?'

'Yes, of course I will, but be careful Ross.'

'I will, I promise. And you carry on as normal and if he gets in touch you don't let on that there is anything you know. Come on, my love, we can't waste a good meal. I'm only sorry I have to get back to Picton tonight, but my place won't run itself and I'm on the brink of some very exciting news. I'll phone you tomorrow.' He insisted on getting her a taxi before he went back to the station, and his goodnight kiss set every pulse in her body alight.

Chapter 29

The police investigating the fire at Nick's Palace had both Nicholas and Maura in for questioning. Someone had told them that she was his girlfriend. They were interviewed separately. Her usual model girl's poise almost deserted her when she was asked if she could think of anyone who might have done this. 'Someone with a grudge against Nicholas Page or you? Someone who is jealous of his success or your involvement with him? A dissatisfied customer or employee or anyone you know who is fascinated with fire?'

'I'm sorry, I can't think of anyone,' she said.

The next question took her completely by surprise. 'Do you have a key to either the restaurant or to Nicholas Page's apartment overhead, Miss Lington?'

'I have a key to Mr Page's apartment because I keep some of my things there,' she said, 'but I don't have one for the restaurant.'

'I see.' His tone and his expression clearly

said he saw more than she had indicated. She was in the interview room for over an hour and had to wait a further fifty minutes afterwards for Nick who was in a different room 'being grilled,' he said later. When he came out to join her he was fuming with anger.

'Practically accused me of setting light to the place myself to get the insurance money. As if I'd do that after all I went through to build it up.' He turned on the young re-porter who was following him out of the building. 'And you can bugger off. There isn't any story of any kind so scarper before I really lose my temper and land you one.' They were in the car and away as the photo-grapher's flash went off. 'Bloody news-hounds, let's get the hell out of here.'

They went to her flat, stopping only to pick up a Chinese takeaway. He strode up and down the small kitchen as she dished up.

'Swarming all over my private life, check-ing my character with the staff at the other places, it's indecent, that's what it is. They should be looking for the real culprit instead of hounding innocent victims.'

She was so tempted to tell him about Jim, but restrained herself. He went home to his flat, 'which the police have very kindly allowed me to use again after their clumsy men have been all over it for clues.'

'Nick, they're doing their job, that's all. There's nothing personal in it, and I'm sure they will apprehend–'

'Well, I'm not. The blighter's probably miles away by now, looking for other properties to set fire to. The only good thing about this is that he didn't use petrol and create a blaze that would have destroyed everything. Probably because he didn't want it discovered too quickly and a slow fire gave him time to get away. He's sunning it somewhere on the Mediterranean now, I shouldn't wonder.'

Not quite as far away as that, she thought, unless that letter and Ross's and my deductions are way out.

Ross telephoned just as she was going to bed. 'Good news, Maura. There's a tramp, for want of a better word, who sort of does the rounds in the area. He often tries to sleep on Salisbury station, but of course the police move him on, although they know he often sneaks back. To cut a long story short, they knew he was, and still is in the area, and they took him in for questioning. With the promise of a good meal and a pint he was very co-operative. He described a man who alighted from the early train and went into the gents. He's quite a smart-looking tramp, apparently, and takes advantage of places where he can have a wash and brush-up. He did this and was back on the platform waiting for the chap who was sweeping up to go back into his office when this bloke emerges from the gents, but he's dressed differently. He has the same rucksack he went in with, but whereas he came off the train in "a black top of some kind and trousers" he is now dressed in "shorts and a bright T-shirt that 'urts yer eyes to look at". The tramp also said he was wearing a wig because he swore the chap's hair was dark when he went in and fair when he emerged. "But it was the same bloke, could tell by the way 'e walked and there weren't no one else who got off and went in the gents".'

'Wow!'

'The police have your uncle's letter to me and they think Jim will get in touch with you. In the absence of an address for him, they want you to play along with whatever he suggests in the way of visits but to let them know. If you can't let them know then phone or text me on my mobile and I'll do so. One or two words will do – something like Jim and the name of the place you are to meet. I'll have my mobile on at all times, day and night. You OK, my love?'

'Yes,' she said faintly, overwhelmed by the turn of events. 'What if he doesn't, though? There's that café he took me to. I'm sure I could find it again.'

'The police seem pretty certain that he will. He'll want to know what is happening, they said, and you are his best bet. Cousinly interest, they said, but of course you know nothing about how far they've got. They also said they would contact you about all this.'

'All right, Ross. I do hope it can be cleared up quickly. I was at the police station here for ages this afternoon while they went over my movements and asked all sorts of questions.'

'I suppose they have to, Maura. Not nice for you, though. Wish I was up there with you to lend some moral support, darling. I can't wait to see you again,' he added. 'Any chance of you coming down? As long as you let the police know where you are I'm sure that would be OK and if Jim is keeping an eye on your movements it could even make it easier for them.'

She shivered at the thought that her cousin might be secretly watching her.

'I'm working tomorrow, Ross. I'll try after that.'

Chapter 30

Maura had two sessions on the catwalk the following day. Since her refusal of Craig Escudo, and definitely since the signing up of the latest model, her presence at high-profile shows had been less frequent. Well, she told herself, I've had it good for quite a number of years and I think I'm ready for fresh pastures anyway. She knew where she wanted her future to be, but Jane was still in evidence in that area, although Ross insisted she was a friend, the widow of a very good mate in Australia. That did not detract from the fact that the woman was staying in Primrose Cottage most of the time. Whatever happened now, her liaison with Nick was finished and she needed to turn her mind towards the manor house and what she was going to do with it.

Cousin Jim was waiting when she came

down the steps of Escudo's at lunchtime. Her insides seemed to do a double somersault. She *had* to get this right. He greeted her as though there had been no harsh words between them. 'I enquired in there earlier on and they said you would be busy until now, so I came back. I want to apologize, you see. About the way I carried on over the will and everything. I don't blame you, Maura, it was just my bad luck that Tom didn't sign that new will. It isn't your fault and I should have been more gracious about it. I'm sorry, Maura. Am I forgiven?'

'Of – of course.' She held out her hand. 'To prove it how about coming to supper with me this evening? It will give us a chance to talk.'

'Your boyfriend won't be there?'

'No, just you and me. I've no appointments tonight and I'll show you that I can cook as well as strut the catwalk.'

He entered into the spirit of the conversation as she had hoped he would. 'You're a real sport, Maura. That guy you're with is lucky.' An idea occurred to her to make absolutely certain he turned up at her flat.

'Actually, well, we've split up. It wasn't working and I don't really want to talk about it, but we aren't together any more.'

He reached out and touched her hand. 'I understand, Maura. I've been in that situation myself. What time shall I come this evening?'

'About six. Would that be all right? Oh, hold on a minute, I forgot to check whether I'm needed in the late afternoon parade for a promotional film we're doing. I don't think I am but I'll make sure. Don't want to leave you on the doorstep for an hour.' She went up the steps and into the building. She phoned the police on the special number she had been given.

'I'm on my way,' Inspector Jonners said. 'Keep him talking outside Escudo's until I arrive. I'm wearing a suit and I'll be carrying a brown leather briefcase. I shall go into Escudo's and that will be the cue for you to finish your conversation with the suspect. Someone will follow him to find out where he lives. I'll be in touch with you later. What time is he coming to you?'

'About six.'

'Right. Just be natural with him. And don't worry when we knock on the door because the building will be surrounded and there will not be any police sirens or lights to give the game away. Surprise is the element here. We are more than halfway to you already so it's safe to go outside again now.'

Although Maura knew this was planned she was more nervous than she thought she would be. She lingered in the building for a few seconds more to give the police time to arrive, then she went back to Jim.

'Sorry, that took longer than I thought. It's OK though, I'm not needed this afternoon. Once you start on an outside shoot you can never be sure what time you'll get away. The one I did the other day took nearly two hours more than planned because of what they called technical difficulties. Being a model isn't all glamour, you know, Jim.'

She saw the man with the briefcase walk up the steps and into Escudo's and gave her cousin a radiant smile. 'I must get off if you're to have a meal tonight. OK? See you later, Jim.'

He touched her hand again. 'Thanks, cuz. I'm really looking forward to it.' He even blew her a kiss as he moved away and she felt awful for a moment. Suppose it wasn't Jim who started the fire in Nick's Palace? Still, she had to go along with this now. She hoped Nick didn't suddenly turn up or phone because she needed Jim to feel totally relaxed. If only Ross were here with me I could cope with it so much better, she thought suddenly as she made her way on to the tube.

Jim arrived at two minutes to six, clutching an exotic looking pot plant. 'I'm not too early, am I?' he enquired. 'I was so keen not to be late that I allowed much more time than I actually needed to get here.'

'Not at all, Jim. Come on in and I'll get you a drink while I check on the progress of our meal. It's a simple cottage pie with fruit and ice cream to follow, and I've a wonderful selection of cheeses from a little shop I know.'

He thrust the plant in to her hands and, feeling a total traitor, she mumbled her thanks, moved a bowl of fruit and placed the plant in the centre of a small table near the window.

'Let me know if I can help at all,' he said as she went towards the kitchen, 'I've done a bit of catering in my time, as I believe I told you.'

'I'm fine. You sit down, relax and make yourself at home.'

They were halfway through their meal when Jim mentioned the manor. 'I haven't told you that I called in when I was in the area the other day, but of course, your Mrs Duffy may have done so. Made me real welcome with tea and home-made cake she did.' He looked enquiringly at her.

'Yes, she did mention it when we spoke on the phone. We must arrange for you to come down when I'm there, Jim. I've been so busy with Esmeralda off sick and me taking on so much more, but it is beginning to be easier now, so we should be able to arrange something soon.'

'That would be great, Maura. Just say the word and I'll pop some things in a case and wallow in the old place for a few days again. I was on a walking trip when I looked in. Couldn't resist, as I was so close. I missed the old manor when I went to Canada, you know, especially at first, but I made good over there, made friends and...' he stopped dramatically and gazed across the table at her. 'Why don't I take you over there with me? I presume you have a holiday sometimes? Show you the sights, you know, and you could stay as long as you wished.'

He was so obvious, she thought. No boyfriend on the horizon now, his chance to get in and eventually get the manor house.

'My work takes a lot of time, Jim, and I can't afford to turn opportunities down. In this career you need to be available. There's always someone else waiting to step into your shoes.' She felt safe talking to him about her modelling rather than the manor house. He hadn't mentioned the fire at the restaurant. She wondered whether the police had got into his house and found any incriminating evidence and she felt guilty at being part of such a deception, yet if he was an arsonist...

Suddenly aware he was speaking to her, she said quickly, 'Sorry, what did you say?'

'That I understand about your career. So let's fix a date for a get-together at the old homestead before I go back to Canada, shall we? I'd like to take some photos of it to show friends back there and to look at myself sometimes.'

'I'll check some dates with my agent and–' The bell rang. She jumped up quickly and went to the front door. She heard Jim say, 'I thought you weren't expecting anyone, Maura.' With her hand on the latch she said loudly, 'I wasn't,' and the next moment Inspector Jonners and another plainclothes man were in the little flat.

As they took Jim away, 'for questioning regarding a fire at Nick's Palace in Oxford Street', he looked back at her. 'You bitch,' he said. 'I'm sorry now that I didn't torch the manor instead of the restaurant...'

They drove off but left a policewoman with

her. 'Thanks for what you did,' she said. 'We found a box of wigs and other minor disguises in his room. And he's just admitted it himself with that remark to you.'

The phone rang and, hesitantly now, Maura went to answer it.

'Hi, Maura. I'm at the tube station. All right if I come along to your flat now?' Ross's voice was warm with concern. 'I gather Inspector Jonners has left. He just spoke to me.'

'Yes, of course, Ross. There's a policewoman here now. They've taken Jim in for questioning.'

'I'll be there just as soon as I can.'

He arrived ten minutes later and the policewoman left.

'Oh Ross, I felt such a heel,' Maura said, 'acting like that when I knew all along what was going to happen.'

He put his arms round her. 'He deliberately set fire to the restaurant, presumably to get even with Nicholas Page because he refused him a job. He would probably have done the same to the manor when he was sure he wasn't going to have it himself. No need to feel bad about what you did. You were brilliant.'

'Perhaps I could get a job as an actress

when the modelling dries up?'

'I've a better idea. Let's sit down and make ourselves comfortable. This may take some time because there is much to tell.'

On the cosy two-seater settee he put his arm across her shoulders, drawing her closer to him. 'I've been in town most of the day, Maura.'

'Any special reason?'

'Several. One, I took Jane to the airport this morning for her flight home. I was sorry you didn't get to know her. Her husband was one of my best friends. He was killed in a plane crash.

'Two, today I concluded a deal to buy the farmland that adjoins Primrose Cottage and I wanted to tell you. It's so exciting, Maura. We were in the estate agents' together the day I began negotiations for it, you know.'

He smiled and stroked her hand with his free one. 'You pretended not to notice me but I knew you had.

'Three, I've had a wonderful idea for your manor house. How about using one room for conferences? Occasional one-day affairs about anything you care to discuss. Farming, modelling, the arts, lectures, courses, whatever. There'd be no need to alter anything. It's all there and it would bring in a

317

bit of money to help with upkeep without disrupting your home. But the most special reason of all is that at last I can ask the girl I love to spend the rest of her natural with me. I'll only be able to kiss with one side of my mouth for a few more days, but I'll make up for that later. Are you willing to risk it my princess?'

She leant over and kissed him, on his cheek, his nose, his forehead, anywhere but that still fragile lip.

The publishers hope that this book has given you enjoyable reading. Large Print Books are especially designed to be as easy to see and hold as possible. If you wish a complete list of our books please ask at your local library or write directly to:

Magna Large Print Books
Magna House, Long Preston,
Skipton, North Yorkshire.
BD23 4ND

This Large Print Book, for people
who cannot read normal print,
is published under the auspices of

THE ULVERSCROFT FOUNDATION

... we hope you have enjoyed this book.
Please think for a moment about those
who have worse eyesight than you ...
and are unable to even read or enjoy
Large Print without great difficulty.

You can help them by sending a
donation, large or small, to:

**The Ulverscroft Foundation,
1, The Green, Bradgate Road,
Anstey, Leicestershire, LE7 7FU,
England.**
or request a copy of our brochure for
more details.

The Foundation will use all donations
to assist those people who are visually
impaired and need special attention
with medical research, diagnosis
and treatment.

Thank you very much for your help.